Mercy doctoring the Bravo Ridge livestock was a safe and sane way to start putting the feud behind them.

Safe. Sane.

What Luke wanted when he looked at her was not safe. And not sane. Not in the least.

He wanted to touch her. To stroke a hand down her shiny black hair, to press his palm against her soft cheek. To taste that ripe, red mouth of hers. And more...

A whole lot more.

What was the matter with him to even consider messing with Javier Cabrera's daughter?

He *wasn't* considering it, he told himself firmly.

Uh-uh. No way.

He took a step closer to her.

Dear Reader,

I've always wanted to write my own Romeo and Juliet story. However, since I write romance, I would write the kind where the hero and heroine *don't* end up dead.

Almost sixty years ago, James Bravo won a hundred acres, including mineral rights, from Emilio Cabrera in a bet on a horse race between Emilio's finest Andalusian and a Mustang that James had caught running wild and trained himself. The land and the rights were the last of a proud family's legacy; the Cabreras, under Spanish rule, had once been Texas royalty.

Since then, the two families have been locked in a cycle of mutual animosity. Blood has been shed on both sides. In recent years, the families have steered clear of each other. Things seem to be working out well that way.

But the shaky peace is about to be shattered—when a Bravo and a Cabrera fall in love.

Happy reading, everyone!

Yours always,

Christine Rimmer

CHRISTINE RIMMER

A BRAVO'S HONOR

SPECIAL EDITION®

Published by Silhouette Books

America's Publisher of Contemporary Romance

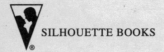 SILHOUETTE BOOKS

Recycling programs
for this product may
not exist in your area.

ISBN-13: 978-0-373-65457-4

A BRAVO'S HONOR

Visit Silhouette Books at www.eHarlequin.com

Printed in U.S.A.

CHRISTINE RIMMER

came to her profession the long way around. Before settling down to write about the magic of romance, she'd been everything from an actress to a salesclerk to a waitress. Now that she's finally found work that suits her perfectly, she insists she never had a problem keeping a job—she was merely gaining "life experience" for her future as a novelist. Christine is grateful not only for the joy she finds in writing, but for what waits when the day's work is through: a man she loves, who loves her right back, and the privilege of watching their children grow and change day to day. She lives with her family in Oklahoma. Visit Christine at www.christinerimmer.com.

For Betty Lowe,
dear friend and devoted reader.
In loving memory…

Chapter One

"Luke! Wake up, man! We got trouble!"

Luke Bravo shot to a sitting position from a sound sleep. He raked his fingers back through his hair and squinted at the bedside clock—2:10 a.m.

And someone was pounding on his sitting-room door. "Luke! Wake up!" Luke thought he recognized the voice: Paco, one of the stable hands. He sounded seriously freaked.

Stark naked, Luke jumped from the bed. Grabbing his hat off the back of a chair as he flew by, he raced through the sitting area. Lollie, the spotted hound he'd raised from a pup, had beaten him to the door. She paced in front of it, whining and sniffing the crack between the door and the floor.

"Back, girl. Sit," he commanded. With a final worried

whine, the dog moved out of the way. Luke yanked the door wide. "Paco. What the hell?"

About then, the housekeeper, Zita, came flying around the corner from the servants' rooms, muttering in Spanish, clutching the sides of a flimsy red robe. She let out a shocked little squeak when she got a load of Luke standing there in the altogether.

He put his hat over his privates. "It's all right, Zita." He aimed a narrow-eyed glare at Paco. "Is there a fire?"

Paco slapped a hand over his mouth to quell a snort of laughter at the housekeeper's embarrassment, and mutely shook his head.

"No fire?" Luke asked again, just to be sure. When the stable hand's head went back and forth a second time, Luke told Zita gently, "I'm on this. Don't worry. Go on back to bed."

Face noticeably flaming, even in the dim light provided by the hallway wall sconces, Zita whirled and ran back the way she had come. A choking laugh escaped the stable hand.

Luke leveled a scowl on him. "If not a fire, then what?"

Paco's grin vanished. His smooth dark face grew somber. "It's Candyman. He cut his ear on something. There's blood everywhere. He's gone loco. We can't settle him down."

Though stallions were rarely even-tempered, Candyman, Bravo Ridge's prize stud, was a true gentleman. A black-footed gray from foundation Quarter Horse lines, he produced top-quality horses for show, ranch work and everyday riding. As a rule, you could count on him to be easygoing and calm.

If he was out of control, he must be hurt bad.

"On my way." He shoved the door shut, put on his hat and grabbed for his clothes. Once he had his Wranglers and boots on, he told Lollie again to stay, as he slipped out the door. He took off, racing down the back stairs and out one of the service entrances into the hot August night. Halfway across the back gardens, he caught up with Paco.

By the time they reached the dirt driveway that circled the main house and grounds, Luke could hear Candyman's screams. He ran faster, Paco close on his heels, across the driveway and around the stables to the prize stallion's paddock.

As they approached the paddock fence, Luke saw that someone had got a rope on him—but hadn't been able to hold it. The rope trailed loose along the stallion's neck. Candyman bucked and snorted. Gray mane flying, he shook his proud head, stomping the ground, sending clods of dirt and grass everywhere. Blood, black by the light of the nearly-full moon, ran down his powerful neck. His eyes shone wide and wild—one filmed with blood from that raggedy, sliced-up ear.

Half-blind and scared to death. Even once he got the animal settled a little, the doctoring required would be beyond Luke's rudimentary veterinary skills. On the other side of the far fence, the stallion's mares whickered and restlessly paced, frightened to see the big gray so far out of control.

"Call Doc Brewer." Luke barked the order over his shoulder at the stable hand. "Tell him to get the hell out here. Now." He climbed the six-foot metal fence surrounding the paddock. As he jumped to the ground within, he gave a low whistle.

The stallion stood still, then, and scented the air.

"Whoa, boy. Easy now…"

The horse made a questioning sound.

"That's right, it's me. Easy there. Easy…"

Candyman snorted and shook his silver mane. But he didn't rear again. He waited, withers twitching, snorting again softly, as Luke cautiously approached.

"Yeah, boy. Good boy…" He held out his hand, palm flat. Candyman gave it a sniff and then allowed him to grasp the dangling, bloody rope.

Luke patted the powerful neck and laid his cheek against it, feeling the tacky wetness of clotting blood. "Come on, now. Let's get you in your stall…."

The horse went where Luke led him, though reluctantly, switching his tail and making low, unhappy noises. Twice, he jerked the lead to show Luke he wasn't the least bit happy about the situation. Each time the horse resisted, Luke would stop and speak softly to him. He would stroke the stallion's fine forehead and blow in his nostrils.

In time, Candyman allowed Luke to take him into his stall. Once there, it was a matter of keeping him settled until the doc arrived—which had better be soon.

Paco appeared on the far side of the stall door. "The doc's in the hospital."

"Tell me you're joking."

"Wish I was. Hip replacement, they said. They're sending his new associate."

Luke would have blistered the air with bad words if he wasn't being careful not to stir up the stallion. "Whoever he is, he better know what he's doing. And he damn well better get here fast." Paco made a low sound of agreement. "Get me a bucket of warm water and a clean rag, will you?" Luke turned his attention back to the horse.

Since he'd raised and trained the eight-year-old himself, Candyman always responded well to Luke's voice and his touch. When one of the other stable hands brought the bucket, the horse even allowed him a little prodding at the injury. But the area was too sensitive to touch without anesthetic. Candyman jerked his head sharply, snorting in warning when Luke tried to mop up the worst of it. He decided the cleaning could wait until Phineas Brewer's "associate" arrived with a tranquilizer.

At least it wasn't as bad as Luke had feared at first. With skillful stitching, it might even heal up good as new. Luke willed the time to pass quickly. He talked softly to Candyman as the minutes dragged by. The horse quivered and chuffed at him. "Easy," he soothed, "Easy, boy…"

Where was that damn vet? The smell of blood and hay and horse filled his nostrils. Sweat beaded under his hat and ran down his bare chest. "Turn on the fan," he commanded to anyone who might be listening. "It's an oven in here…."

Someone flipped a switch and the stall fan spun.

Softly, in order not to spook the injured horse all over again, he spoke to Zeke, who ran the stables and now hovered close on the far side of the stall door with Paco and three other men. "Your men find what caused this mess?" Candyman's stall and paddock were carefully constructed to be both secure and smooth-sided. A stallion, even a calm-natured one, was more curious and sensitive to his surroundings than other horses. Special care was taken to protect against sharp nails or any projection on which the prize animal might injure himself.

"We found a board knocked down in the run-in shed." The run-in shed, located on the far side of the stallion's paddock, was an open shelter the horse could use to get out of the sun or sudden bad weather. "A big nail was exposed, the head broken off and bloody from where he hooked his ear on it."

"Is it fixed now?"

"You bet."

Luke heard the crunch of tires on gravel in the driveway outside. "That the vet?"

"I'll get him." Zeke hustled off and returned an endless couple of minutes later. "It's the vet, all right."

Candyman stirred and snorted nervously. Luke patted the horse's neck and spoke in a slow, careful tone. "Get him in here."

"It ain't a he."

Luke glanced toward the stall door. Through the pipe bars, he saw the new vet.

Clearly not a he.

She met his surprised glance, a fine-looking woman, full-breasted in a white t-shirt. Her smooth olive skin was scrubbed clean of makeup and her long black hair, parted in the middle, was tied back in a low ponytail.

It was her eyes that held him, though. They were cat-slanted and black as midnight. He remembered those eyes. "Mercedes?"

She nodded, a graceful dip of her dark head. "Hi, Luke. How you been?"

He shook his head. Time did fly. "Little Mercy Cabrera…"

One of the hands muttered something appreciative. Another one laughed. Someone whispered darkly, "Cabrera…" Everyone knew that a Bravo never trusted a Cabrera—and vice versa.

Luke commanded, "Enough," and the men were silent. He spoke to Mercedes. "I remember hearing you went off to college."

"I did. Eight years ago."

Damn. Had it really been that long? "You, and then Elena."

"That's right." Her sister, Elena, a Cabrera by blood, was three or four years younger. "We're doing all right, both of us. Moving up. I graduated from A&M. You'll be relieved to know I passed my national veterinary board exams with flying colors." She carried a black bag. And she looked…plenty capable. It was something in the tilt of her strong chin, in the intelligence shining in those striking eyes. Damn. Little Mercy Cabrera. Adopted into the Cabrera family when she was twelve or thirteen. It seemed to him she'd been sixteen just last week. Sixteen, meaning jailbait…

She sure looked full grown now.

"Time goes by," he softly observed.

"Yes, it does. I'm partnered up with Phineas since last month. He wants to retire in the next few years. I'm going to do my best to fill his shoes." She stepped close to the bars and spoke in a quiet, even tone. "Need some help with that horse?"

Candyman's nostrils flared as he scented her. But he didn't flatten his good ear or swish his tail, a fair indication that he would tolerate her tending him.

"Cut his ear up pretty bad." So what if she *was* a Cabrera, and good-looking enough to have him thinking things he shouldn't? Candyman needed doctoring and she was the only vet present. "You think you can stitch him up for me?"

"Can you keep him settled while I have a look?"

"Come in here. Do it nice and slow."

So strange, Mercy thought, to be there in that stall with Luke Bravo and that beautiful, bloodied stallion in the middle of the night. Since she first came to San Antonio with her poor, doomed mother fourteen years before, she'd had a crush on the tall, golden Bravo boy. She'd seen him riding a fine horse in a parade once. And at the San Antonio winter stock show and rodeo, the big one, that used to be held at the Freeman Coliseum.

For most of her teenage years, the rugged young Anglo had filled her girlish fantasies.

Not that it could ever be more than a foolish girl's day-dreams. She was as much a Cabrera now as if she'd been born one. And no self-respecting female in her family would go out with a man who had the last name of Bravo.

The Bravos had stolen much from her people. The land she now stood on, this ranch the Bravos had re-named Bravo Ridge, had belonged to the Cabreras for hundreds of years—until Luke's grandfather stole it from Emilio Cabrera back in the fifties. One Cabrera man had lost his life slaving for the Bravos. And another, fighting them.

"What's his name?" she asked Luke.

"Candyman."

"Good with the ladies?"

"A gentleman, always."

The horse allowed her touch. He whickered softly into her palm. She performed a quick examination just to make sure there was nothing more to treat than the bloody, half-hanging ear.

"Well?" Luke asked, as she finished the exam.

She wished he'd worn a shirt as she tried not to stare at his sweat-shiny, blood-streaked, perfectly formed male chest. "I'm going to have to medicate him before I can clean and stitch him. Can you lead him out of the stall for me?"

He nodded. So Mercy unlatched the door and backed into the main part of the stable. Luke started to bring the stallion out, too. But the horse grew fractious, jerking the rope Luke had on him, blowing hard through his nostrils.

Luke was gentle. And so patient. He petted the stallion and whispered in his good ear. When he guided the horse forward again, the animal went quietly.

Mercy had the needle ready. As Luke petted and soothed the big gray on one side, she thumped the other side of the horse's neck sharply with three fingers to desensitize it. She was good with a needle, got it in quick and smooth. Swiftly attaching the syringe, she gave the injection and eased the needle out. Candyman didn't seem to feel a thing.

Luke stayed close, petting the horse and talking softly to him, as the drug took effect. After a few minutes of waiting, he sent a glance around the stable at the watching men. "We gonna need these boys, you think?"

By then, she had judged that a local anesthetic should do the trick, since Candyman seemed settled and kind of peaceful, with the trank in his system and Luke stroking him and whispering to him.

"I think the two of us can handle this now," she said. "As long as help's in shouting distance if there's trouble."

"Go on back to your bunks, boys…."

The men left them.

Mercy had the second injection ready. The horse snorted softly when she gave him the shot just behind his ragged ear. But he was already relaxed from the tranquilizer and she was done so fast, he never got around to kicking up a fuss.

As they waited for the area to grow numb, the horse was calm and the stable was quiet. All the stalls were empty, which didn't surprise her. In the hot summer weather, the horses would be happier and more comfortable outside during the night.

"It's so quiet," she said, feeling strangely self-conscious.

Luke made a soft sound of agreement.

"You live in the main house?"

"I do."

"The rest of your family, too?"

"Uh-uh. Most of them have houses in San Antonio. Or elsewhere." Luke had six brothers and two sisters. "But they all come back to the ranch for holidays and to get away from the rat race now and then."

She shook her head.

"What?" he asked in a whisper, a smile playing at the corner of his finely-shaped mouth. "Some reason I shouldn't live there?"

"All those fat white pillars. Like a palace in Greece. Or maybe a Southern plantation house."

Luke chuckled low. "You would have had to know my Grandpa James. He modeled it after the Governor's mansion."

Once the Cabrera hacienda, La Joya, the jewel, had stood where the huge white house with those proud white pillars stood now. Mercy had seen pictures of La

Joya and thought it so fine, so suited to the land it was built on, with thick stucco walls and a tile roof to keep things cool in the hot Texas summers. James Bravo had torn the hacienda down to build the white mansion surrounded by green lawns and rose gardens.

"Must cost a small fortune to water all that grass," she said, keeping it offhand, not allowing any bitterness to show. She was, above all, loyal to her adopted family. But now was not the time to raise the specter of the longtime blood feud.

He kept things neutral, too, with a half-shrug of one powerful bare shoulder. "We use well water. What can I tell you? My father loves that damn house and those rolling green lawns maybe more than my grandfather did."

She touched the horse, sliding a hand down his neck first, and then carefully reaching up again to press the flapping, bloody flesh of his torn ear. Candyman didn't flinch. "He's ready. I need to wash my hands."

"Over there."

She went to the long, deep concrete sink at the far wall and lathered up with the strong disinfecting soap in the tray there, then dried her hands with a paper towel from a wall dispenser. Luke watched her, she knew it. She could feel those eyes of his, searing a hole in her back, tracking her every move. She tossed the towel into the wastebasket by the sink and turned again to face the man and the stallion.

For the stallion's sake, she approached them slowly. And maybe, if she were honest, it wasn't only that fine gray horse that had her moving with care. Something in Luke's burning blue gaze made her pulse turn slow and lazy, made her heart beat a deep, hungry tattoo beneath her breasts.

He had blood on his cheek. In a sudden, shocking image, she saw herself licking it off.

"Tell him nice things," she instructed, "and keep a soothing hand on him. I'll need to clean him up first."

Luke was impressed with Mercy's doctoring skills.

Fifteen minutes after she washed her hands, Candyman was clean and stitched up and bedded down in his stall, with the fan going to keep the heat of the night at bay.

And Mercy Cabrera was putting her instruments away in that black bag of hers, getting ready to leave.

Luke didn't want her to go.

Which was insane. And also stupid. Where could it go with the two of them? Nowhere. If he made a move on her, he would only be asking for trouble.

There hadn't been a flare-up in hostility between their families in years. Not since his father hired her adoptive mother, Luz, to work for him in a well-meaning attempt to put the old feud to rest.

Davis Bravo's plan had backfired. Luz's working for a Bravo had infuriated her husband, Javier, who had demanded his wife quit immediately. She hadn't. Things had gone downhill from there.

Since then, the families had sense enough to avoid each other. It had been going well. Tensions were low enough that a little minor interaction would probably work out fine.

Mercy taking over for Phineas…that could be good. She could treat Luke's horses. But she wouldn't technically be working *for* anyone named Bravo. There would be nothing in such a transaction to get Javier Cabrera's back up again, nothing to poke at that hot-headed pride of his. Mercy doctoring the Bravo Ridge livestock was a safe and sane way to start putting the feud behind them.

Safe. Sane.

What Luke wanted when he looked at her was not safe. And not sane. Not in the least.

He wanted to touch her. To stroke a hand down her shiny black hair, to press his palm against her soft cheek. To taste that ripe, red mouth of hers. And more...

A whole lot more.

There were a bunch of pretty women in South Texas who didn't have Cabrera for a last name. If he wanted companionship he should go looking for one of them. What was the matter with him to even consider messing with Javier Cabrera's daughter?

He *wasn't* considering it, he told himself firmly. Uh-uh. No way.

Mercy hooked the clasp on her black bag and stood. "The stitches are the kind that dissolve, so I won't need to remove them. But I'll come by next week to check on him."

"Thanks." The word came out rough and low. All he had to do was nothing. Just stay right where he was until she was gone.

He took a step closer to her.

Her dark eyes widened. Another step, close enough that he could smell her. She smelled good. Fresh. Like a meadow of wildflowers in early morning. With a hint of something sweetly spicy, something exotic and tempting.

"I, um..." She licked those lips of hers, quickly drawing her pink tongue back inside. He wanted to sink his teeth into the smooth brown flesh of her throat, to suck that tongue of hers deep into his mouth. To rip off that snug T-shirt, shove down those faded jeans. "Call the office," she said. "If there's a problem."

"I'll do that." He held her gaze and his voice went lower, rougher. "I remember you. When you first came to stay with the Cabreras. I remember those eyes of yours. Black. True black."

Those eyes tracked—his mouth to *his* eyes. And back again. "She had cancer, my mother."

"I heard that. It was hard for you, huh?"

"She died a year after we came to stay with Luz and Javier. They made her final months as good as they could have been. They loved her. And me. And I'm their daughter now, their true daughter. In my heart. And by law."

He stepped closer. Close enough he could have reached out and grabbed her. But he didn't.

She held her ground. "I owe them everything."

Another step. He was crowding her. There was no excuse for such behavior. But he did it anyway, stepping sideways, boxing her in. Too late, she moved to put distance between them. Since he blocked the exit, she backed up. Three steps and she could go no farther. The section of wall between Candyman's stall and the next one over stopped her. She watched him, her eyes locked on his, as he closed the distance between them.

"Luke."

"What?"

She gazed up at him, eyes deep and dark enough for drowning, and she whispered, "We shouldn't…"

Before he took her mouth, he whispered back, "I know."

Chapter Two

She sighed when his lips touched hers. It was the sweetest, sexiest sound. A sound of surrender. A sound that told him everything he needed to know.

The black bag fell to the straw at their feet.

He wrapped his fingers around the bars of two stalls—Candyman's and the empty stall next to it. He did that to keep from grabbing her, to keep from pulling her down to the straw-strewn dirt floor with him, to control himself.

At least a little.

He held those bars hard and tight as he kissed her, nuzzling those soft, sweet lips of hers, urging her to open and then sliding his tongue inside the instant her lips parted.

She tasted so good. He drank in her long, hungry sigh, then lifted his head from hers just long enough to slant the kiss the other way. That time, she let him inside without his even having to press his tongue against her lips. She parted for him and he swept those silky, wet inner surfaces.

Her low moan of need and desire had him pressing his hips to her, rubbing his aching hardness against her flat belly.

Too soon, with a low cry, she turned her head away. "No," she whispered. "No..." Her breath came hot and heavy.

So did his.

Her hair tangled against the stall bars, and her dark lashes were down, silky fans against her smooth cheeks, those eyes closed to him. And she kept her head turned hard away. Luke's mind got the message, though his body didn't like it. With slow care, he peeled his hands from around the bars and stepped back from her.

Only then did she turn her head to him and open her eyes. Her lips were redder even than before, plundered by his kiss. And her eyes had storm clouds in them. With stunning grace, she dipped to her knees and grasped the handle of her vet's bag. She rose again with the same elegance. Luke stepped to the side, clearing her way out of the stable.

"That never happened," she said flatly. And then she turned and left him there.

Luke watched her go, aching to follow, to grab her and kiss her again.

But he knew she was right. It was asking for trouble to even consider getting something going with a Cabrera. And he *wasn't* considering it. He would be steering clear of the tempting Mercy from now on.

* * *

"He did not." Elena's big brown eyes were shining.

"Oh, yeah. He did."

"Did you…like it?"

"*Chica,* don't ask me that." It was Thursday night, less than twenty-four hours after Mercy had stitched up Luke Bravo's gray stallion. Elena was spending the night at Mercy's little South Side house. They sat on Mercy's bed, sharing secrets the way they always did, with Mercy's dog, Orlando, snoozing on his rug in the corner. Mercy was sitting cross-legged behind her sister, brushing Elena's long, brown hair. So beautiful, her sister's hair. Softly curling, crackling with life, silky to the touch and shot with strands of red and gold. "I would love to have your hair, Elena…."

Elena reached back and stilled Mercy's hand. "Who cares about my hair? I want to know if Luke Bravo's a good kisser."

Mercy freed her hand from Elena's grip and continued brushing. "It doesn't matter."

"Tell me. I mean it."

Mercy couldn't hold back a laugh. "*Papi* would kill me."

"Tell me." Elena scooted out from under Mercy's touch and turned to face her.

"I shouldn't have mentioned it."

Elena sucked in a breath of pure sisterly outrage. "What? Of course you should have mentioned it. You should tell me everything. Same as I tell you."

"I told him no. When I left, I said that it never happened."

Elena lowered her head and glanced up from under her lashes with a slow grin. "But it did. And you liked it."

Mercy set the brush on the nightstand. "Yeah. I liked it. I liked it a lot. Way too much. And that's why it can't ever happen again."

Elena scowled. "That's stupid. You *like* him. I can see it in your eyes. In the way your face goes all soft when you talk about him."

"He's a Bravo. His grandfather stole our land, tore down our home and killed our grandfather. Then he murdered our uncle. And his father caused *our* father to leave our mother."

"James Bravo didn't steal our land. His horse beat grandfather's horse in a race. James Bravo bet money. And grandfather bet La Joya because he wanted that money and the rancho was all he had by then. And then grandfather died on a Bravo oil rig, working to support his family, since he'd foolishly gambled his home away."

Mercy had her mouth hanging open by then. "What's the matter with you? Now you're defending the Bravos?"

"It's a stupid feud. We both know it. James Bravo killed Uncle Emilio in self-defense."

"That's what the Bravos said. And the Anglo sheriff went along with his lies…."

"And *Papi* shouldn't have been such a jerk when *Mami* took that job with the Bravo company."

"How can you know that, Elena? You weren't even born then."

"I know *Papi* left *Mami* until Davis Bravo fired her and made him feel justified again for hating anyone with the last name of Bravo. I love Dad. But he shouldn't have done that. All she did was get a job. This is America. A woman has rights, too."

Mercy put her hands against her cheeks, assumed a stunned expression, and teased, "I am shocked, Elena. Shocked."

"Joke about it all you want. You know I'm right. It's time to put an end to this feud. Time peace was made. And if you like Luke Bravo, I don't see why you can't go out with him."

Mercy made a low sound of disbelief. "Seriously. It's a bad idea and it would only make trouble—and I have to say, since you got back from California, you've turned into a real hothead." Elena had recently graduated from UC Berkeley with a major in American history and an education minor. She would take her first teaching job in the fall.

"I do see things differently now," she said. "I see that *Mami*'s gotten rich selling houses and condos. And *Papi*'s doing just fine with Cabrera Construction." Elena was right. Luz and Javier had started with nothing and built their very own American dream. Even with the housing downturn and the various crises in the mortgage industry, the Cabreras had the reputations and client base to stay afloat in tough times. "They need to put their old prejudices behind them. It's not like they're all downtrodden and suffering anymore. The old animosities just hold them back."

"Maybe so. But they still wouldn't like it if I went out with Luke. I don't want to hurt them. I couldn't stand to do that."

"If they're hurt, that's *their* choice. They could choose otherwise. And they don't get to be the deciders on *your* life. They just don't. *Es su vida.* Your life, not theirs. You have to stand up, Mercy mine. Stand up—and I will stand with you."

Mercy reached out and guided a thick coil of brown hair back over her sister's slim shoulder. "My sister, the firebrand," she said fondly.

"And proud of it," Elena replied, a certain determined gleam in her eyes. Mercy knew that gleam. It meant trouble. She would trust her sister with her very life. But she should never have been so stupid as to tell Elena about kissing Luke—and liking it. "I have an idea," Elena announced. "And don't look at me like that. It's a killer idea. Saturday night. You and me. We're going to Armadillo Rose. And we are going to dance and do us a few shooters and have a fine time."

Armadillo Rose was a great local bar in Southtown, a few miles north of where Mercy lived. They had live music on the weekends and the bartenders were all female and expected to be outgoing, willing to jump up and dance on the bar. It was owned and run by Corrine Lonnigan—which was why Elena had that gleam in her eye. Luke's brother, Matt, was the father of Corrine's only child. From what Mercy had heard, Matt and Corrine got along great, though they had never married. And Matt's brothers and sisters were always welcome at Corrine's bar.

"Oh, no," said Mercy.

"Oh, yes," said Elena. "Don't give me any arguments. We are going."

"If you have plans to hook me up with Luke, you're destined for disappointment."

"We'll see about that."

"Come on. What's the chance he shows up there the same night we do? Very small."

"See? Nothing to worry about, then. We'll have a good time and you won't have to make a choice between what you want to do and what *Mami* and *Papi* expect of you."

Luke kept thinking of Mercy.

Of the taste of her soft lips, the smell of her skin. It was damn distracting when he had a horse ranch to run and an estate to manage. More than once in the days right after that night in the barn, he would find himself staring into space when he should have been going over the oil leases or concentrating on the early training of a valuable foal. He checked on Candyman often, watching that stitched-up ear real close. Once or twice, he half-wished that ear would get infected so he would have to call Mercy back before her scheduled visit the following week. A man was in big trouble when he wished his prize stallion ill.

He knew he needed to get her off his mind, needed to get out and get himself some feminine companionship. Someone pretty and sweet and not a Cabrera.

His brother Caleb dropped by Saturday evening. Caleb was a salesman by nature *and* profession, the top producer at the family company, BravoCorp. He could sell a homeless man a bedroom set. Their dad was always offering him a management position. Caleb didn't want to manage anything. He thrived on sales. He had a moody Balkan housekeeper named Irina and a new girlfriend every night.

The brothers had dinner together in the main dining

room at the long mahogany table that could seat the whole family during holiday celebrations.

"It's lonely in here with the just the two of us." Caleb glanced around at the heavy, carved furniture, the three crystal chandeliers dangling from the twelve-foot ceiling and the striped silk wallpaper. "We should have eaten in the kitchen or out in the sunroom."

Luke shrugged and sipped his wine and ordered the image of a just-kissed Mercy to get the hell out of his head. "It's fine."

His brother looked at him sideways. "You seem distracted. Something on your mind?"

"Not a thing."

They ate in silence for a few minutes. Then Caleb set down his fork. "It's too damn quiet. Let's go out."

Maybe that wasn't such a bad idea. He might meet someone. Get his thoughts off Phineas Brewer's new associate. "Like where?"

Caleb pushed back his chair and tossed his napkin down beside his half-finished plate. "Who knows? We get in the car and we drive. We see someplace interesting, we stop. We keep our options open. It's more fun that way."

Since Bravo Ridge was on the southwestern edge of the Hill Country, they went north first, and found a dance hall in Bandera. They had a couple of beers and danced the two-step with a pair of secretaries down from Austin for the weekend. Luke wasn't exactly enjoying himself. The girl he danced with was a pretty little blonde wearing too much perfume. The point was to get his mind off Mercy, but instead, he found himself making comparisons. The blonde did not come out ahead.

Around nine-thirty, Caleb tapped him on the shoulder. "Let's move on."

Luke tipped his hat to the blonde and followed his brother out. They got back into Caleb's brand-new black pearl Audi R8 and rolled the windows down as they raced along a couple of twisty ranch roads, finally meeting up with I-10, and heading south toward San Antonio. By the time they got to Southtown, Luke had figured out where his brother was taking him.

Caleb swung into the packed parking lot.

"There." Luke pointed at a pickup that was just pulling out. Caleb eased into the free space and killed the powerful engine. They could hear the music from the rambling tin-sided building. A big neon armadillo with a red rose tucked behind its ear graced the place of honor over the wide main doors.

Caleb winked at him. "I'm in a mood to kiss Corrine and watch a pretty woman dancin' on the bar."

Elena laughed as she slid back into the chair across from Mercy. Her cheeks were flushed and her brown eyes shone. She'd danced just about every dance since they claimed their table an hour before.

Mercy had danced, too, though not as often as her baby sister. And she'd had a Corona and a shot of Cuervo Gold. She had a slight buzz on and she should have been happy. She was out with Elena and the music was good. And there was very little chance Luke Bravo would come strolling through the big double doors.

"You look sad." Elena flipped a shining coil of hair back over her shoulder and put on an exaggerated frown.

"I'm not," Mercy lied. "I'm having a great time." She raised her Corona and took a sip.

Elena's expression brightened. "Well, cheer up, *mi hermana*. All your dreams just came true." Mercy followed the direction of Elena's gaze.

Luke.

He'd just come in with one of his brothers. Incredible. She'd been so sure she was safe, that he would never show up while she and Elena were there.

She turned back to her sister. Fast. "I don't believe this is happening."

"Believe it." Elena beamed. "And smile. They're coming this way."

Caleb nudged Luke in the ribs and leaned close to be heard above the music. "Over there. That's the Cabrera sisters, I'm sure of it."

Luke turned his head slowly. Mercy had her back to him. But he could see Elena. And he would have known Mercy, anyway. Anytime. Anywhere. Already, he'd memorized the shape of her shoulders, the exact color and texture of her crow-black hair, which was loose and softly curling down her back.

He should turn around and leave. Now. Just march the hell out of there.

Caleb had other ideas. "We ought to be friendly, don't you think? I mean, what's the point of all that old animosity? Let's go say hi to them."

"What the hell for?" Luke growled. But Caleb already had hold of his arm and was dragging him across the scuffed wood plank floor. Luke dug in his heels. "What we ought to do is leave them alone."

Caleb hesitated. "I just want to say hello."

"Forget it. Let's get a drink, say hi to Corrine."

"You can relax." Elena's eyes sparkled with mischief. "They went over to the bar, after all."

Relax? Impossible. Mercy's heart beat so hard, she felt faintly sick. She wanted to leave. And she also wanted to get up and go to him, to pull his mouth down on hers and stick her tongue down his throat. It was embarrassing to feel like this. Like she had no control of herself, like she was an animal driven by the most basic urges. Mercy loved animals. She'd dedicated her working life to them. But she didn't want to behave like one.

"Care to dance?" A nice-looking guy in cargoes and a crew-neck shirt stood by the table, smiling down at her.

"Sure." Mercy put her hand in his and let him pull her to her feet. As he led her toward the wide cleared space, she glanced back to see that another guy was leading Elena onto the floor.

It was a line dance. Mercy knew the steps well enough to keep up. More than once, she and Elena passed each other as the lines separated and reformed. Elena would brush her shoulder or nudge her with an elbow and then toss her head in the direction of the long bar, where Luke sat facing out, nursing a beer.

Watching.

Mercy was careful never to let her eyes meet his. She focused on the steps of the dance and smiled at her partner and told herself to forget Luke Bravo, to enjoy the music and have a good time.

As the song ended and her partner thanked her for the

dance, she couldn't resist a glance toward the bar. Luke wasn't there. A girl in a purple camisole and a black miniskirt sat on his stool sipping a frozen pink drink.

Mercy felt ridiculously bereft. Had he left, then? Or was he asking some other girl to dance?

She shouldn't care. She *didn't* care. Another guy caught her hand. "Hey. Dance?"

She forced a smile and the band started up again. A two-step. Her partner held her lightly. They exchanged names. He said he was in the air force, stationed at Lackland. She told him, half-shouting to be heard over the music, that she was a large animal vet. He said he had a German shepherd named Duke. He had a feeling Duke would be getting sick real soon....

She laughed and explained that she mostly cared for livestock.

"Well, then, I guess I need to buy me a cow."

When that dance ended, he asked for another. He seemed nice enough, but she had a hunch he would be asking her out next. Maybe that would have been good—to go out with a nice guy, maybe get something going.

But it didn't seem right somehow. She wasn't really interested. She'd only be using him in an attempt to forget about Luke.

So she shook her head and went back to the table where Elena waited with a couple of fresh beers. She slid into her seat.

Elena glanced past her shoulder. "Don't look now, but he's on his way over here."

Mercy frowned. "The guy I was just dancing with?"

"No. Luke."

Mercy's heart leapt, but she spoke calmly. "You said that before. Didn't happen." She picked up her beer and took a long, cool sip.

"It's happening *this* time."

Mercy glanced over. And there he was. Impossibly tall and too handsome for words, standing right by her table.

Elena beamed a big smile at him. "Luke Bravo. How you doing?"

Mercy faced forward, staring blindly in front of her as he and her baby sister exchanged inane pleasantries. She picked up her beer again and took another sip. A long one.

That was when Luke said, "Mercy, how 'bout a dance?"

Yes, she had expected that. Still, she almost choked on her beer. With great care, she set the bottle down and swallowed. Elena grinned at her, triumph and challenge lighting her eyes.

Mercy's pulse raced and her face felt flushed. But really, she was making way too much of this. What could it hurt? It was only a dance.

She turned and laid her hand in Luke's.

Wouldn't you know it would be a rare slow one? Luke took her in his arms, careful of her as if she were fine china, delicate and breakable. Strangely, at that moment, she *felt* as if she might break, brittle and confused—and still, even though he held her lightly and not too close, terribly aroused by his nearness.

Her lips tingled. They longed to feel his kiss. And her cheeks felt so hot, burning, as if with fever.

He said, "I swear, I didn't plan this."

She realized she'd been avoiding looking at him and made herself meet those sky-blue eyes, accepting the shock of heat that went through her as their gazes connected. "It's okay. Really."

"Only a dance, right?" His words echoed her thoughts. Was he trying to convince himself, too, that a dance was all this was?

She made a small, nervous noise of agreement and glanced away. Elena danced by, in Caleb's arms. Mercy gaped in shock and Elena beamed her a big, wide smile.

Was it just her imagination, or was the world as she'd known it spinning fast out of control?

Only a dance, she reminded herself silently. She closed her eyes and let the music take her, let herself enjoy this forbidden moment, with Luke's arms holding her in that special, cherishing way, with the warmth of him and the scent of his aftershave tempting her, with his cheek against her hair.

It was over too soon. He stepped back and his mouth quirked in a beautiful, rueful smile that pierced her straight to the heart.

"I know," he said softly. "This dance never happened."

"You've got a thing for Mercedes Cabrera," Caleb said with a low chuckle as he drove them back to Bravo Ridge.

Luke stared out the windshield at the dark ribbon of highway in front of them. "You don't know what you're talking about."

"I saw the way you looked at her—the way *she* looked at you…" He made a sizzling sound through his teeth. "Hot enough to melt steel."

"Mind your own business, little brother."

"You going out with her?"

"Hell, no."

"Why not?"

"Don't pretend to be naive. We both know you're anything but."

Caleb drove in silence for a while. Luke almost dared to hope the topic was dropped. It wasn't.

"The feud is ancient history," Caleb said. "What's it to us? We're a whole new generation. We ought to try and get beyond the old garbage. You know, heal the breach. It's been years since—"

"Tell all that to Javier Cabrera."

"If *I* wanted to go out with Mercy, I wouldn't let anything stop me." Caleb fiddled with the radio, turning it up, listening for a moment, turning it down again. Finally, he said way too casually, "Elena grew up to be gorgeous, didn't she?"

Luke did look at him then. "You're not serious."

"She's cute and fun. And smart. And I like her."

"Don't do it, Caleb. I mean it. Why take the chance of stirring up trouble? It's not worth it."

Caleb sent him a puzzled glance. And then he shrugged. "All right. If it bothers you that much, I won't ask Elena out."

"Good. Don't. Leave it alone."

Wednesday at four, Mercy showed up at the ranch. She drove straight to the stables, as Luke had figured she would.

He was there when she arrived. He'd been hanging around the horses all day, telling himself it was a good idea to be there, that it didn't hurt to spend some time with the men now and then, to see how they were handling the mundane daily work.

It was crap, his reasoning. Just an excuse. He knew his men and he had chance enough day-to-day to make sure they were all on top of their work. The real reason he was at the stables all day had shining black hair and eyes to match. He hadn't known when her rounds would bring her there.

And he wanted to see her.

Since Saturday, he'd tried to stay with his plan to forget about her. It wasn't working out very well.

He'd started thinking how some things only got more powerful the more you denied them. And that maybe Caleb was right. In the end, the feud had nothing to do with their generation.

Luke saw her drive up. He told Paco to bring Candyman into his stall for her. "And ask her to stop in at the house when she's done."

At Paco's nod, he went out a side door, Lollie at his heels. He moved swiftly across the back lawns to the same service entrance he'd used that night a week before. In the house, he sent the dog to her bed in the corner of the kitchen and took the wide central hall to the front foyer, where he lowered himself to one of the carved benches, skimmed off his hat and set it down on the bench cushion beside him.

He waited, feeling like he was about to burst out of his skin, for sixteen minutes. And then, at last, the doorbell rang. He rose and answered.

She had her hair tied back again, like that night last week. Even in the shade of the deep front veranda, it had a shine to it. She carried a purse instead of that black bag. He allowed himself a slow, hungry look, starting at her booted feet and moving up over her long, slim denim-clad legs. She wore a short-sleeved green shirt that buttoned down the front. And her mouth was set in a mutinous line.

"Hey," he said, stepping back to usher her in just as Zita appeared to answer the door. She saw he had it handled and turned back the way she'd come. He said to Mercy, "Come on in."

She didn't budge. "Your horse is doing fine, healing up fast. And I know you have an account at the clinic so we don't have to discuss the charge. You'll get a bill, same as always."

He thought about kissing her again. And more. Not only sex, either. He thought about reaching out, taking her hand, leading her across the threshold and over to the bench where his hat still waited, right there in the foyer. He thought about sitting her down and asking her to talk to him, to tell him everything about her. What she loved. What she hated. Her favorite color. Whether or not she liked broccoli. Why she'd decided to become a vet.

"It's not about the bill," he said quietly. "You know that."

"Luke." Her voice had gentled. "I really need to go."

"Do you like broccoli?"

She blinked. Twice. "Excuse me?"

It came to him then. What to do. How to approach this. "One date. That's all. We'll go somewhere nobody knows us. We'll…talk."

"Talk." Her soft mouth curved. It wasn't a smile. "Right."

"How do you know this isn't something important?"

She frowned. "Important?"

"That's right. We've both been thinking how we'll regret getting anything started, how between your family and mine there's never been anything but trouble. But what if we've got it wrong?"

"Wrong…"

"Yeah. What if the regret will come from not even trying, from not even giving each other a chance? What about that?"

Her mouth had softened. And so had those night-dark eyes. "I…I've wondered that. I have. Especially since Saturday night."

"One date. We'll see how it goes, find out if it's all wrong, or if maybe this is something we shouldn't pass up, no matter the risk, no matter the possible consequences."

She tipped her head to the side, kind of studying him. "You think we're going to learn all that in one date?"

He answered honestly. "Maybe not. But it's a step."

A long moment passed. Finally, she took a card and a pen from her purse. She wrote on the back of the card and then held it out to him. "Park around the corner. I'm a big coward. I don't want to hurt my mother or my father. For now at least, I just don't want them to know about this."

He took it. And he read what she'd written. "I'll be there," he said.

Chapter Three

It was well after dark when Luke got to Mercy's South Side neighborhood that Friday night. He'd taken one of the pickups from the ranch. It was a dull green and dirty, the wheels, side panels and front grill spattered with mud, the kind of vehicle no one would look at twice.

Mercy didn't want anyone to know about the two of them. And he was willing to go along with that—at least for now. He parked two blocks from the address she'd given him, and walked the rest of the way, past small houses with dry patches of lawn in front and chain-link fences. Even after nine at night, the August heat was punishing. He heard the steady drone of window air conditioners. Here and there people sat on their front porches, laughing and talking. The occasional car rumbled by, giant speakers blaring out rap music or Tejano.

He kept his gaze front and his feet moving, feeling slightly ridiculous, thirty-one years old and sneaking around like a misbehaving teenager. But then he smiled to himself. Like a teenager in more ways than one. He glanced down at the bouquet of red roses he had picked from the garden himself. All tied up in knots, hormones on overdrive, on his way to see a certain special—and forbidden—girl.

When he turned onto her street, he slowed his steps and checked addresses. In the glow of a porch light he made out a number—203. Her house was number 212. It would be across the street.

He found it easily in the light of the streetlamp, a neat little cottage, blue with white trim. Geraniums grew along the fence and a rose trellis masked the concrete front porch. No garage. That pickup she drove waited in the narrow driveway between her house and the next one over.

Luke stood beneath the spreading shadow of an oak on the cracked sidewalk across the street, clutching his handful of roses, and staring at that little blue house, telling himself he could still change his mind. He was a simple man, really. He liked steak and baked potatoes. He said what he meant. His word was his bond. He believed in his parents' longtime successful marriage and his family in general and loyalty and love, though you would be unlikely to catch him running his mouth off about that stuff.

He wondered what he was doing there, why he had insisted that she give the two of them a chance. He considered turning and going back the way he'd come.

But his desire—both to have her and to know her— was simply too powerful. He was a practical man in the grip of something he couldn't control, something he doubted he would ever understand.

It was no good trying to convince himself to walk away. Desire held him there, stronger than all his compelling arguments to the contrary.

Luke emerged from under the shadowing branches of the tree and crossed the street. He went through the gate and up the three steps to her door.

He raised his fist to knock. But before he made a sound, the door swung open and her hand came out. She grabbed his wrist and pulled him inside, shoving the door shut again the second he crossed the threshold.

Since she was so close, he slipped an arm around her and brought her closer. He looked down into her upturned face, drinking in the sight and scent and feel of her. She had her hair down, blue-black and shining, and she wore a loose-fitting blouse that had slid off one shoulder.

"You're beautiful." He whispered the words, reverently.

Her strong chin quivered. "I've been…so anxious. Longing for you to be here, wishing you wouldn't come, praying that you would. Going back and forth like a seesaw."

"I know the feeling." He pulled her nearer, wrapping both arms around her, heedless of the roses, which he held against her slim back. She didn't resist him, not this time, only curved against him, warm and soft, all woman. A perfect fit.

She reached up, touched his face, her eyes full of wonder. "Oh, Luke. My heart is beating so hard…."

"Mine too. So hard…"

He kissed her. He *had* to. Hungrily, he speared his tongue inside, yanking her up hard and firm against him, pressing his hips against her, letting her know exactly how she affected him. His blood pounded in his ears, so loud the sound filled up the world.

When he lifted his head, she sagged against him, as though the kiss had made her legs too weak to hold her up.

He tried to control himself, tried to think of something other than how much he longed to take off all her clothes and lay her down on the couch across the room and make love to her all night long. "I wanted...I thought we would talk, you know? Learn about each other..."

She laughed low, and the sound seemed to vibrate along his every nerve. "How's that working out for you?"

"It's not." With a low groan, he took her mouth again. He was like a starving man—starved for *her.* For the feel of her, the taste. For all of her...

That time, she was the one who broke the kiss. She put her hands on his shoulders and dug her fingers in, shaking him a little, making a hissing sound between her white teeth. And while she shook him, she looked up at him, lips soft and red, eyes so very serious.

He met her gaze, frowning, not sure what her expression meant, what she might be thinking.

Her hand slid down his arm and she caught his free hand. "Come on. To my kitchen. We'll put my table between us. It will be easier to act like civilized people that way."

Obedient as a well-behaved child, he followed her through the arch at the far side of the living room. Her kitchen was small, with a brightly tiled counter, a two-seater table, and a pair of bentwood chairs painted yellow. She pushed him down into one of the chairs.

It seemed about time to offer the roses. "I picked these for you. The color made me think of you. Red. Like your lips when I kiss you."

She put the pads of her fingers against her mouth, lightly. He wanted to be those fingers, touching that mouth. He had to will himself not to surge up out of that chair, grab her in his arms and kiss her again.

And again…

She took the flowers from his outstretched hand. "Thank you." She brought them close and breathed in the scent of them. "Mmm. Not like the ones you get at the store with all the fine, dewy rose smell bred right out of them." She turned for the cupboard and brought down a yellow ceramic pitcher painted with daisies. As she filled it with water at the sink, a scraggly three-legged dog limped in from the other room.

The dog stumped right over to him and wagged its raggedy tail. "Hey." He let the mutt sniff his hand and then scratched him behind the ears. The dog dropped to his haunches and stared up at him adoringly.

Mercy turned from the sink. She unwrapped the roses from the newspaper cone he'd carried them in and arranged them in the pitcher. Then she brought the arrangement to the table and set it in the center.

"His name's Orlando." She gave the dog a fond glance. "Someone dropped him off at the clinic a year ago. He'd been in a car accident. They amputated his crushed leg, patched him up and, since no one would take him, they let him live there. Until I came along and couldn't resist those sweet, hungry eyes. I adopted him. Or maybe he adopted me…"

"I've got a dog. Lollie. She's a sweetheart." Feeling

suddenly awkward and inexplicably tongue-tied, he petted the dog some more as she went to the fridge and got out two beers. She opened them and returned to the table, where she took the empty chair.

Holding his gaze, she slid one of the bottles across to his side. "I told Elena that you kissed me. That I...couldn't stop thinking about you."

"When did you tell her that?"

"Before we saw you and Caleb at Armadillo Rose." She ran her finger down the side of the sweating bottle, wiping a path in the condensation as she went. "It was her idea, going to Corrine's bar Saturday night. I said how that was silly, that you and I had agreed it was not going to happen between us, and there was almost no chance you would show up there, anyway. So then she asked me what I was afraid of. And I went, just to prove I wasn't scared—and also because, deep in my secret heart, I was hoping you might be there." Her dark lashes swept down. When she looked at him again, she added, softly, "And you were."

He loved her eyes, that slight, sexy slant they had, their velvety blackness. "I wouldn't have been there that night, except for Caleb. He decided we needed to get out. He drove. I just settled back and went where he wanted to go."

She slid her beer across the table until it clinked against his, then she pulled it back. "Would you call that fate?"

He watched her smooth throat as she drank. "I'm glad that you were there."

She set the bottle down again. "Elena thinks the bad things between our families are in the past, that we all need to move beyond what happened so long ago, that it's got nothing to do with us, with our generation."

He'd guessed as much from the way Elena behaved the other night, greeting him with a smile, dancing with Caleb. "But you feel differently."

As she considered what he'd said, the dog, Orlando, rose wearily to his three feet and limped away into the living room.

Finally, she spoke. "The other night in the stable, I did feel differently. All I could think then was that going out with you would only be a betrayal of everyone I love. But after listening to my sister lecture me about how the animosity between our families is all in the past…" She touched the pitcher with his roses in it, then brushed her finger across the velvety petals of one of the blooms. "Maybe I've been making a big thing out of nothing. Maybe it really is all over and done. My dad used to speak of your family with anger. With disgust. He really hated your grandfather. And your dad, too. But in the past few years, he hardly mentions you Bravos. He and my mom are happy, doing well."

Luke thought of his own father. He wondered how Davis Bravo would react to him and Mercy getting together. The old feud aside, Davis had big ambitions. He wanted his sons to marry rich Texas debs, to bring connections and fat fortunes into the family. So far, it hadn't worked out that way. Ash had married a store-keeper from California. And Gabe's new wife was a poor Hill Country widow. How would Davis take it if his third son married a Cabrera?

Marriage…

Whoa. He was getting way ahead of himself. He had spent maybe an hour in Mercy's company, total. They hardly knew each other. He needed to remember that.

She said, "You're so quiet, all of a sudden. Is something wrong?"

He sipped from his beer—and sidestepped her question. "Saturday night on the way home, Caleb said he was going to ask Elena out."

She gave a disbelieving laugh. "You're kidding me."

"No. I talked him out of it. Now I'm thinking maybe I shouldn't have. Not on account of the family feud, anyway."

"But for some other reason?"

He shrugged. "Caleb is such a damn player. He's almost as bad as Gabe was before he met his new wife, Mary. He might break poor little Elena's heart."

Mercy made a scoffing sound. "You don't know my sister very well."

He had to admit, "No, I don't." He studied her amazing face. "I have a lot of questions."

"Like what?"

"Why did you become a vet?"

She pulled the pitcher of roses close, breathed in their scent, then pushed them back to the center of the table again. "The usual reasons, I guess. I love animals. And I'm good with them. They like me, they feel safe with me."

Lucky animals. Luke didn't feel safe around Mercy. Not safe at all. "Are you dating anyone?"

She looked at him so solemnly. "Now? No."

He couldn't help asking, "But you were, recently?" When she nodded, he pressed her further. "Did you love him?"

"Love…" A frown formed between her sleek black brows. "I thought so. For a while. We were together in veterinary school. Until about six months ago."

"What went wrong?" Luke's voice was gruffer than he had meant for it to be.

"I don't know. How does that happen? It all seems right and then slowly you start to see it's not going to work out, that it's not a forever kind of thing, after all."

"Did you bring him home, to your parents?"

"I did, once. They liked him."

"Where is he now?"

"He went back to Kansas, where he was born and raised. His dad's a vet, too, so he'll be taking over the family practice."

"You're still in touch with him?"

She laughed that low, husky laugh of hers. "Luke Bravo, are you jealous?"

Damn straight. "No."

She tipped her head to the side and her hair spilled over her shoulder, like a black waterfall. "No, I'm not in touch with him. It seemed better that way. Just to let it go."

A certain tightness in his chest eased away. "Where did you live before you came to stay with the Cabreras?"

Another laugh escaped her. "Hold on a minute."

He scowled. "What?"

"What about you? Any special girlfriends?"

"No. No one special."

She smiled then, a slow smile. "Well. Okay, then."

He asked again, "Where were you born?"

"California. Salinas. My dad was a farm worker. He died when I was five, stabbed to death in a bar fight. My mother tried her best to support us, working as a maid in a motel. She did okay for a few years. Then she got sick. My mom—Luz, I mean—was like a sister to her.

They grew up in Corpus Christi together. Javier sent the money and we came to stay here." She made a low, wondering sound. "Luz and Javier. Where would I be without them? They *are* my mother and father, every bit as much as my birth parents were. They love me and they raised me as a true daughter. They gave me a chance to go to college, to make a good life, to own my own house and pay my own way." Tears shone in her eyes.

He hadn't meant to make her cry. "Mercy." He rose to his feet. "Don't cry…."

She dashed the tears away. "Sometimes it's good to cry, when there's deep emotion."

"Good to cry…"

"Yes." She gazed up at him, the tears still there, glittering like diamonds in her eyes.

He reached down a hand. She laid hers in it. He pulled her upward and wrapped his arms around her. He stroked her silky hair, kissed the smooth skin at her temple. She rested her head on his shoulder with a soft sigh. For several long, sweet seconds, they stood there by the table, holding each other close.

But then she raised her head and captured his gaze. "I would like…not to say anything to anyone else. Not for a while. I'll tell Elena to keep silent. And we could just see how it works out with us."

His heart leapt. He wasn't sure about taking this thing with them public, either. But he wanted to keep on seeing her. He wanted it bad—so bad he ached with it. And now she'd admitted she wanted it, too.

"All right," he said. "For a while."

"We'll…be together when we can. Just the two of us." She stared up at him, her expression grave.

"Yes."

Was it the coward's way? Probably. But then again, time for just the two of them, what could that hurt? This was all so new. And they had no way to know where it would go from here. Right now, with her in his arms and the scent of her tempting him, it seemed impossible that what he felt would ever die. It seemed she belonged with him, forever. But it could end, just fade away, as it had with her and that guy from Kansas. It could turn out that there'd been no need, after all, to take the chance of stirring up trouble.

She took his shoulders, pushed him away a little. "Here I am in your arms again. Somehow, lately, I always end up here."

He gathered her closer. "I don't want to let you go."

She rose up on tiptoe and offered those rose-red lips to him. "Kiss me again, Luke. Kiss me a hundred times."

He took her mouth in a long kiss that stole his breath and sent the blood pulsing hot through his veins.

When he lifted his head, she whispered, "I have a confession."

"Tell me."

"When I was a girl, I saw you once, in a parade, riding a white horse."

"I remember that parade. It was after Thanksgiving. The holiday parade…" It must have been before her mother died. He had spotted her, a skinny kid with huge black eyes, picked her out of the crowd because she seemed to be staring so hard at him. Later, he had asked around about her, found out she was staying with the Cabreras.

She said, "After that, I dreamed forbidden dreams of

you. I dreamed of this. I dreamed that you would be my lover." She laughed. "Well, I was only twelve. Maybe lover is the wrong word. My sweetheart, I guess. My boyfriend…"

Her loose cotton shirt had fallen down her shoulder again. He touched the glowing, silky skin that the shirt revealed, hardly daring to believe what her words seemed to mean. "What are you saying? What are you telling me?"

"I'm saying I…I want you, Luke. Maybe I have since that first time I saw you. I'm saying…ah, this is crazy, huh? I don't *know* what I'm saying. It's only that when you touch me, when you kiss me…it's like my little-girl dreams all come alive for me. At last."

It seemed only fair, only right, to make a confession of his own. "I remember you, too. Your black eyes that seemed to see right through me. Even when you were a skinny little kid, I noticed you. And then, about the time you turned sixteen…" He let the words trail off.

She slid her hands to his shoulders and gave them a shake. "What? Tell me. What?"

"I saw you once, with your girlfriends, at the rodeo." His voice sounded rough to his ears. It was partly arousal. And partly a deeper emotion, one he wasn't prepared to give a name. "You were laughing at something, your head thrown back, black hair shining in the lights. And then you saw me watching you. Your laughter stopped. Your face changed…"

She gave a slow nod. "I remember that night. I felt so strange when you looked at me. Scared. And yet also very powerful, very much a woman."

"Mercy. You were sixteen."

"But I didn't *feel* sixteen. Not when you looked at me the way that you did."

He ran a finger down the smooth flesh of her neck. "I knew I had to keep clear of you. I knew you were dangerous. And not only because I was twenty-one and you were underage. Not only because your last name is Cabrera."

Her dark eyes sparked with challenge. "But here you are, Luke. In my house. With your arms around me…"

"Yeah, here I am. What the hell's going on with us? Why is it I never want to leave?"

"I have no answers," she whispered. "Only more questions."

He bent his head, pressed his lips to the fragrant skin of her shoulder. She shuddered under that caress and he pulled her closer. He took her mouth again. She melted into him, as if her body knew his, had always known, as if there was some magical, absolute affinity between them, as man and woman, as if the attraction—the *need*—was bred in the bone.

When at last he lifted his head, he waited for her to open her eyes, for her long, sooty lashes to rise. She stared up at him, dazed, red lips wet from their kisses.

He knew he could have her, right then and there. He *ached* to have her, to peel off that loose cotton shirt and those tight jeans. To take away everything, all the barriers between them. To see her naked. To touch her all over.

To take her here, in the kitchen, on the table. Or up against the ancient yellow refrigerator. To lead her into her bedroom, lay her tenderly down on the pillows and bury himself deep in her softness. To kiss her all over, to bring her to climax once and then again. And again.

Until she begged him to stop—and then pulled him close and demanded he do that some more.

More. Yes. For their first time, he wanted more than just tonight.

"Come away with me," he whispered. "Give us some time, together."

She ran a finger along the crew neck of the shirt he wore. He felt her touch like a brand. And she asked, "Isn't that what this is now, tonight? Time, together?"

"I want more. All night. And the morning after. I don't want to be interrupted by daylight. I don't want to have to sneak off before dawn."

"Oh, Luke. Where would we go?"

"There's a place I know in the Hill Country. North of Fredericksburg. A cabin on ten acres. We use it when we want to get away…."

"We?"

He tipped her chin higher with a finger, brushed his lips against hers, felt her breath, sweet and warm, against his mouth. "We Bravos. The family."

"When would we go there?"

"This weekend—all weekend. I'll pick you up on Friday afternoon. And I'll bring you back Sunday evening. Can you get away?"

"I think so." Her gaze held his, unwavering. "Phineas isn't on his feet yet and won't be for a while. But we have other vets we trade off with for emergency calls."

"Do it, then. Get the time off and come with me this weekend."

Chapter Four

Mercy had no trouble getting things set up at work.

But after she arranged for the time away and agreed with Luke that he would pick her up at the clinic at three Friday afternoon, she felt a little guilty—mostly for running away with a Bravo. But also for going off without telling anyone in the family. What if her mom or dad dropped by her house while she was gone? What if, God forbid, there was some emergency and they needed to reach her?

Yes, she knew it was all just guilt talking. They could call her cell phone if they needed to talk to her. And if for some reason, they couldn't get through on the cell, they could call the clinic. She'd instructed the weekend receptionist *and* the night switchboard to give her family members the number at the cabin, where Luke said they had recently put in a landline.

Really, she kept telling herself, all they had to do was call if they needed her. She could be back home in less than two hours.

But no. The real issue ran deeper than any worry that they might need her when she wasn't there. She couldn't shake the feeling that her actions were a betrayal of her mother and father, of all they had done for her, of their love and their trust.

In the end, she couldn't stand it. She called her mom at work and said she was taking the weekend off. She gave Luz the number at the cabin and said a friend had offered her the use of a cabin in the Hill Country. When Luz asked who she was going with, she hesitated, snared between the frantic urge to lie and the need to be truthful. But then Luz got a call she had to take. Saved by the bell. Mercy told her mom she loved her and hung up.

And felt worse than ever. More of a liar. Worse of a cheat. Why had she called Luz at all if only to lie to her?

She called Elena.

Her sister crowed in delight. "You have an amazing time, *chica,* and don't worry about a thing. If Mom asks, I'll cover for you—I mean, since you're so sure you need to keep it a big secret."

"She won't ask. I called her and told her I was going."

A small gasp of surprise. "You said you were going away for the weekend with Luke Bravo?"

Mercy muttered guiltily, "Not exactly."

"If not exactly, then what?"

"I said I was going away to a friend's cabin. She got an important call before I could explain who the friend was."

Elena snickered. "Coward."

Mercy nobly sniffed. "We discussed it, Luke and me.

We're going to keep it between us for a while. That's our right, if we want it that way."

"Did I say it wasn't?"

"Elena. You didn't have to say it. I can hear it in your voice."

"What about later?"

"Later, we'll see…"

Elena sighed. Elaborately. "Well, at least you're admitting you want to be with him and you're not letting what happened years and years ago stop you."

Mercy made an impatient sound. "You make it all sound so simple. And why not? You're not the one who can't stop thinking about a Bravo."

Elena scoffed. "If I wanted to go out with one of them, I would. No big deal. And I wouldn't be running around hiding it from *Mami* and *Papi*."

Mercy thought of what Luke had told her the night before. "Would you go out with Caleb?"

Elena answered breezily. "Sure. He seemed fun. He's not a bad dancer. And he's very charming."

Mercy envied her little sister right then. If only she, Mercy, could speak so lightly about Luke. She started to tell her sister that Caleb wanted to ask her out, but then decided not to. She had a feeling Elena might go after Luke's brother if she thought he was interested— not because she wanted him so much, but more to prove her point about putting the old feud behind them. Why give Elena a chance to stir up unnecessary problems?

Elena said, "Have a beautiful weekend, Mercy mine. Enjoy your new love."

"I didn't say it was love."

Elena only laughed. "So defensive. But it's okay.

Just have a good time. *Olvídese sus problemas.* Promise me that."

"I will. I promise."

Luke was waiting beside a shiny red four-door extended-cab pickup when Mercy left the Brewer Veterinary Clinic the next afternoon. A shorthaired hound waited in the backseat, wet nose pressed to the side window. At Luke's urging, Mercy had brought Orlando. He hopped along behind her when she came through the glass doors of the clinic.

Luke looked her up and down, a glance like a long caress. "Your stuff?"

She told her silly heart to stop throbbing and gestured toward her pickup two spaces over. "I'll get them—Orlando. Stay." With a whine, the dog stopped where he was.

Luke followed her to the pickup and took her suitcase from her. He put it inside the fancy camper shell that covered the bed. "I'm thinking if the dogs get along, they can ride in the backseat together. If not, I'll put Lollie in the camper."

She smiled at him. "Orlando's not proud. He gets along. He's no alpha."

"Lollie can be possessive." He looked doubtful.

"Let's give it a try."

"Fair enough."

He opened one of the rear doors. "Lollie. Sit." The dog obeyed. He hooked his fingers in her collar. "Take him over to the other door and put him in, but keep a hold on him. Let's see what kind of a reaction we get."

Mercy knew her dog. He was not a fighter. But she

understood Luke's caution. A dog fight would not be an auspicious beginning to their romantic getaway. She went around and opened the far door and hoisted Orlando up. "Be nice, now." She kissed him on his wiry head. Gentleman that he was, he lay right down and panted happily, his one front paw hanging over the edge of the seat.

"Lollie, down." Luke's dog dropped to her belly. She gave Orlando a disinterested sniff.

And that was that. Orlando wasn't in her space and he didn't challenge her in the least.

Mercy grinned across at Luke. "Shall we go?"

They put the city behind them.

It was a dry year, but the rolling Hill Country terrain was still beautiful, thick with live oaks, dotted with limestone rock formations and the rolling gold grasses of cattle ranches.

They reached Fredericksburg within the hour. It was a pretty little town established by German immigrants a century and a half ago. Beyond the town, they passed a small vineyard, green and lush under the hot Texas sun.

Luke turned down a narrow road and they drove on for several minutes. He turned again and they rode up a hill, the road unpaved and twisting, the oaks arching over it, making a green, dusty tunnel.

At last, the land opened up and they were in a pretty little clearing. She saw the pine cabin, with its rough front porch held up by unfinished beams, two rustic blue-painted chairs inviting them to sit and enjoy the shade in the hot afternoon.

Luke parked in the cleared dirt space beside the

cabin. They got out and let the dogs loose. Lollie bounded off. Orlando ran the best he could, sniffing the ground, hobbling along, happy to be free. They stood by the pickup and watched them.

He asked, "Will Orlando stay close to the house?" When she nodded, he said, "Lollie's good about that, too." He reached for her hand and they twined their fingers together.

It all felt so natural, and right. The two of them, here, in this pretty, private spot. He raised their joined hands and kissed her knuckles, one by one.

And then he pulled her into the warm, safe circle of his arms. She went to him eagerly, lifting her face to him there in the dappled shade of an old oak. They kissed, a sweeter, slower kiss than the urgent ones they had shared before.

When they pulled apart, she lingered in his embrace. His arms held her loosely at the waist and she rested her hands on his broad chest. They were grinning like a couple of very happy fools.

He led her up to the porch and unlocked the cabin door. It was lovely and cool within. There were three large rooms. A living room/kitchen combination, a bedroom with an enormous four-poster bed and a bathroom with both a shower and a deep claw-footed tub.

"The best of both worlds," he said. "Country, but comfortable. All the conveniences, including central heat and air. There's even Dish network TV."

She gazed admiringly at the kitchen, with its rustic cabinets and oilcloth-covered table—*and* up-to-date stainless steel appliances. "I didn't even think about buying food."

He opened the refrigerator. It was full. "We have a

caretaker, Oscar Hoffman. Lives in Fredericksburg. I called him and his wife went out and did the shopping."

She heard Orlando's whine. Luke opened the front door. The dogs sat side-by-side out on the porch, their noses pressed to the screen.

Luke chuckled and pushed the screen wide to let them in. They set out water bowls for each of them. Then they unloaded the pickup.

It took only a few minutes to unpack. Out of the corner of her eye, she saw him take the box of condoms from his bag and put it in the nightstand drawer. She'd brought some, too, just in case he forgot. Since one box was probably enough, she left hers in her suitcase. They slid their bags under the big bed and then they stood on either side of it, staring at each other.

She whispered, "I don't really believe we're doing this…."

"Believe it." His voice was low and rough. "Come over here."

The look in his eyes told her everything. A hot shiver skidded along the surface of her skin.

She went to him, her limbs suddenly heavy, her steps slow. When she stood in front of him, she thought this was it. It was happening. *Really* happening. She was going to make love with Luke.

He clasped her waist. Through the cotton fabric of her shirt, she felt his intent in the way that he touched her, a claim and a caress at once. As if she could ever mistake what was happening here. All she had to do was meet those sky-blue eyes of his to know what was in his mind—what he wanted.

It was so simple. He wanted her. And she, him. Here,

alone with him, away from everything that defined them as Bravo and Cabrera, they could be simply a man and a woman, drawn to each other, free to take their mutual attraction wherever it might lead.

He let his hand trail upward. Mercy sighed as he touched her, palm flat, in the valley between her breasts. He leaned down, gave her lips a brushing kiss. But then he lifted his head again. He unbuttoned the first button at the top of her shirt. And the next. And the next after that.

When he had all those buttons undone, he peeled her shirt wide. "Mercy," he whispered, as he kissed her again, guiding the shirt off her shoulders and away.

He undressed her, as she stood there before him. He took it all, everything. Her shirt and her metal medallion belt, her jeans and her tennis shoes. Her bra and her panties.

She felt weak in the knees and very naked. But then he bent and kissed her breasts, lightly biting the nipples, then sucking them into his mouth. He circled his tongue around them. She clutched his golden head close and forgot all about her nakedness. In an instant, she was a flame, burning high and bright. And he was only too happy to feed the fire.

He dropped to his knees before her and whispered her name again, "Mercy…"

She speared her fingers into his thick, silky hair and bent to press her lips to his. When she released his mouth, he moved closer and kissed her belly, circling her navel with his tongue. She moaned and let her head drop back.

But then she *had* to look again—at his golden head, there, at her belly. He turned his face to the side and laid his cheek against her.

Oh, the feel of that. This was heaven, surely.

"The scent of you," he whispered. "I can't get enough of it...."

He nuzzled the thick, black curls at the top of her thighs. She let out a low cry and braced her legs apart for him.

He wasted no time. He touched her with those knowing, work-rough fingers, spreading her, revealing all her secrets. She was wet for him...so wet.

She was a river. An ocean.

He kissed her, there, in her most secret place, his fingers curving around behind, driving her higher, while with his lips and tongue he found her center—swollen, slick and ready for him.

Hungry.

For him...

She shattered so quickly, tossing her head, growling deep in her throat. She couldn't stay upright, so she let herself fall back across the wide bed. He followed, never losing his hot, wet grip on her, urging her thighs wide, continuing to kiss her, there, where she needed him, as her climax went on and on.

It was like a wave. A powerful, overwhelming wave. It rose up over her, claiming her completely, blotting out everything, drowning her in pure sensual release.

When her completion finally spiraled down to a glow of satisfaction, she lay without shame, limp, legs wide and dangling over the edge of the bed. She knew he could see everything, all of her.

And she was glad. Proud. He was hers, he always had been. From that moment at the rodeo a decade ago—no. Before that, even. From the first time their eyes met, when she was only twelve. A thin, sad child about to lose her mother, a child with a deep loneliness in her heart. The sight of him then had brought hope to her. A promise. A golden promise…

All her worries and her uncertainties were nothing. This was the man who was meant for her.

How could she fear now? How could she doubt?

He rose to his feet and undressed swiftly, holding her lazy-lidded gaze the whole time, tossing his clothing away, as if he couldn't get naked fast enough.

Ah, Dios, he was beautiful. A beautiful man. His arms so strong, the muscles clearly defined, kissed by golden hairs. His chest was thick with muscle, the hair there darker, a deep, rich, bronze color. It grew across his hard pectorals and down in a very kissable trail over a flat, ridged belly.

He was hard for her. Wanting her.

She knew he would take her quickly now. There would be no slow caresses. Not this first time.

This first time would be wild and fast.

And she wanted that. She *needed* that. She scooted back on the bed, shaking her wild hair out of her eyes, crooking a finger to beckon him.

It was all the encouragement he needed. He came down to her, covering her. She wrapped her legs around his hard hips, rocking until she felt him, there, where she wanted him.

He surged into her with a deep, needful groan. Ah, the feel of that. Of him. Within her at last.

And then he said her name again, twice.

She bit his earlobe, growling her pleasure. "No mercy here…"

He rode her. She took him. Deep, so deep. She

answered every thrust with eager movements, her hips rising to meet him, retreating, but only to rise again, inviting him deeper, offering him more.

Oh, how he filled her. A perfect fit. She had him within her and she would never, ever let him go.

They rolled so they were on their sides, facing each other. And then he rolled again, taking her to the top position. She rose up, working her hips on him, taking him so deep, bending her head down so her hair made a black curtain to shield them from everything but their mutual pleasure.

"Mercy…" He said her name again and then he pulsed up into her, lifting his hips up, giving her that last delicious length, that glorious thickness. She pushed down, her climax finding itself in the hot release of his.

She curved her body over him, kissing him as the pleasure bloomed wide, until she could no longer hold herself above him. With a long, shivering sigh, she sank down upon him and he gathered her in.

In time, there was stillness. She slid to the side and laid her hand over his heart, rubbing her palm in the crisp bronze hair, feeling the hard muscle beneath—and also his heartbeat, slowing. And the movement of his chest as his breath flowed in and out.

He caressed her shoulder, then brushed her tangled hair out of her eyes. "Mercy, Mercy…"

They laughed together, the mingled sounds low and so sweet to her ears. The cool air of the room was musky with the scent of their loving.

He pressed his forehead to hers. "Happy?"

She nodded, her throat suddenly tight with emotion. Happy didn't even begin to describe this…this wonder.

This glowing, sweet, sexual beauty. She never wanted it to end. She wanted to lie there in that bed with him, naked and sweaty in the aftermath of their lovemaking, until the last day of the world.

Hasta el fin de tiempo.

Until the end of time.

Chapter Five

This, Luke thought, was a damn good moment.

He had Mercy naked in his arms. And time stretched ahead of them, hours of it—days. Two nights. Two days. Without interruption, without the need for secrecy, without the nagging concern for family loyalty, without having to wonder how it was all going to work out in the end.

Now, this weekend, was an end in itself.

Luke wasn't like Caleb, who took life so lightly. Or like Matt, fourth born, who buried himself in work. Or like Jericho, the family rebel, who had lived to rock the boat and ended up doing time for it. Luke had always thought of himself as the grounded one, the one who knew his job in the world as the keeper of the home-place—knew his job and did it well. A man who loved the land and respected it. A man who loved his family, a Bravo to the core.

But here, alone with Mercy, away from it all, he could lose himself in her, forget his own beliefs about himself. Here, with Mercy, it was all wide open. No loyalties to cling to. No responsibilities to take him away from her or call her from his side.

She seemed to read his mind. "Two days of heaven," she whispered, lifting up on an elbow, bending close to press her sweet lips to the center of his chest. With a sigh, she rested her head over his heart.

He stroked her hair, combing his fingers through the thick, blue-black strands, reveling in the feel of her body pressed to his, one full breast flattened against him, her slim, smooth leg thrown lightly across his thighs.

"Mercy…"

She lifted her head and their eyes met. He did love that feeling, that rising, needful feeling. Like a magic spell woven between them every time he looked at her. It shocked him a little. How much he wanted her. How willing he was to get lost in her black eyes. A man of the earth, he'd never wanted to fly. Until Mercy lifted him up and took him so high.

"Kiss me." He knew the Spanish word for it. *"Béseme."*

She levered up so they were face-to-face. And she kissed him, arousing him all over again, with her scent and her lips and her warm, strong, slim body.

He rolled her under him with a groan, easing his hand between them, testing her readiness. She was wet. Slick with her need for him. He urged her thighs to part and settled between them, positioning himself to claim her a second time. She gazed up him, eyes lazy-lidded, mouth soft with arousal.

And right then, before he sheathed himself for the

second time in her willing softness, he realized he'd forgotten the condom.

Both now. And before.

She must have read his expression. The lazy, sensual glow left her eyes. "Luke? What?"

With a groan of disbelief, he eased off of her.

"What's the matter?" She sounded so scared.

He never wanted to scare her. He cradled the back of her head and kissed the tip of her nose. "I don't believe I messed up like this…."

She shoved at his shoulder. "Like what? Luke, you're freaking me out."

"I forgot to use a condom."

She gasped, those dark eyes going darker still, and muttered something low in Spanish. Then she buried her head against his chest. "*Ay.* I'm so embarrassed. I saw you put them in the drawer, even brought a box of my own. I should have thought…"

He stroked her hair. "Me, too." He kissed the crown of her head. "I'm so sorry."

She looked at him then, cheeks flushed, eyes wide. "It's not your fault—or at least, no more than it is mine."

"You're not angry?"

"Of course not. We got carried away. It was stupid. But we can't turn back the clock. We'll just have to be extra careful from now on. It was only one time…" She sighed. "Okay. Two, if we include just now." She was right, of course. It was possible she could get pregnant from the intimate contact of a moment ago. Maybe not likely. But possible. "We're probably worrying about nothing," she said. "I doubt that I could get pregnant right now."

Was she saying it was the wrong time of the month for her? "Why not?"

"I was on the pill, with Jack." Her cheeks colored again. "It just seemed…the best way."

He didn't want to hear about Jack—but he did want to know about her, about what made her tick, how she saw the world. "The best way to what?"

"Well, I wanted to be with him and I didn't want to take the chance of having a baby when I never knew, really, how it would work out for us. But it's not…how I was raised, you know?" She shook her head. "But neither is this, is it? You and me. Not only am I having sex without being married, I'm having sex with a Bravo."

He suggested, tenderly, talking as much to himself as to her, "Maybe you have to live by your own beliefs, not your parents'."

"I know that. And I do live by my own beliefs. But Luz and Javier, they matter to me. They matter so much. And in some ways they're just so innocent. They married young. They're so…truehearted. Neither of them would ever be with anyone else, no matter what. They're good Catholics. And the hardest thing for them was not to have had a whole bunch of kids. Only Elena. And then me, eventually. I think my dad's always been sad about that. And it has hurt his pride—as a man, you know? That he couldn't give my mom a bunch of children. But still, he stayed true to her and she to him. They both believe that if you want to have sex, you should get married and then pray that God gives you a houseful of babies."

He brushed her hair back from her face with tender fingers. "Times change."

"Yes, they do." She was blushing again. "And I guess that was a lot more information than you needed, huh?"

"Anything you want to tell me, I want to hear." He couldn't quite keep himself from asking, "Jack would be the guy from Kansas?"

"Yes. And what I was trying to tell you, before I veered off into the history of my family, is that I only went off birth control a couple of months ago, four months after Jack and I broke up. I don't know why I stayed on it so long." She gave a small, nervous laugh. "I haven't…been with anyone else until now, until you. Eventually, I decided it was dumb to keep pumping hormones into my body when there wasn't any need…" She glanced away, then forced her gaze back to him. "And here I am saying too much again. I only meant that it can take a while for the effects of the pill to completely wear off. So we might be protected, after all."

"Gotcha."

She brushed his shoulder, a hesitant touch. "You don't like to hear about Jack, do you?"

He admitted it. "No. I don't want any guy touching you but me."

"Oh, Luke. You don't have to worry about that. I don't want anyone but you."

"Good."

"I'm jealous, too," she said softly. "I would hate to hear you went out with someone else."

"There's no one but you." Why would he want another woman, when he could have Mercy in his arms?

She regarded him so seriously. "Are we fools, to talk about being true to each other, when we have no way of knowing if right now, this beautiful weekend, is all we'll ever have?"

A change of mood was in order. He sat up, held out his hand. "Come with me."

She looked doubtful. "Come where?"

"I want to show you my…bathtub."

She laughed then. He drank in the musical sound of it. "I saw it already. It's beautiful. A classic. Nice and long. And deep."

"Share it with me?"

She put her hand in his.

He took a condom into the bathroom with them and set it by the tub, just in case. A few minutes after they got into the water, he was glad he had. He stood up, water and bath-oil bubbles sluicing off him, just long enough to put it on.

Then he sank down into the steamy bath again and settled her onto his lap. She took him inside her with a low moan. Water sloshed over the tub rim as she rode him, her breasts shiny-wet, the nipples like tight little plums, begging for him to taste them.

He couldn't get enough of her. She was like a drug, the sweetest kind of addiction.

After the bath, he found her in the kitchen, cutting up a salad to go with the steaks the caretaker's wife had left for them. He came up behind her and smoothed her hair to the side so he could kiss the vulnerable nape of her neck.

She turned in his arms, a sharp paring knife clutched in her fist, and whispered teasingly, "Don't mess with me, Luke Bravo…" The invitation in her eyes made him hard in an instant.

He took her wrist, pried the knife free and set it, very carefully, in the sink.

She sent him a hot look from under her lashes. "Now you're in trouble."

"Oh, I sure hope so."

She'd put on a short little wisp of a robe after their bath. No underwear. Or at least, he hadn't seen her put any on. But just to be sure, he decided to check. He backed her up tight against the counter.

"I'm starting to feel cornered," she said in a lazy tone, sliding her hands up his chest and resting her arms on his shoulders.

He eased up the robe and found nothing but silky, smooth skin all the way. "No panties. Good." He nipped her earlobe.

She made a low sound, like a purr, deep in her throat. "I think you're planning to seduce me again."

"You think right." He kissed the tender flesh of her throat. She smelled of flowers and temptation. He could eat her right up, savoring every bite. She offered her mouth and he took it, kissing her deeply.

When they came up for air, he slid a condom from the single pocket of the sweatpants he was wearing.

She looked down at it in his hand. "Ah. Good thinking."

"I try. Though I have to admit, with you, it's pretty hard to keep my wits about me."

"Give it to me."

"I intend to."

She laughed low, and took the condom from him. "Drop the sweatpants."

He did, shoving them down, kicking them free of his feet. By then, she had the wrapper off. She curved her hand around him. It felt so good, he groaned. And she played with him, caressing him with slow strokes. He watched her, watched the movement of her slim, shapely hand wrapped around him, working him, taking him higher, making him moan again.

And again.

He was in her control, and all too happy to be there. He'd forgotten all about how he was supposed to be the one calling the shots. She urged him back a step and then she sank on bent knees.

He looked down and thought he had never seen anything quite so beautiful as her hand around him, positioning him, her hair like a curtain of midnight against the white silk of her robe.

She kissed him, drawing him deep.

He thought he would die, then. Die a very happy man.

He watched her take him in and slowly let him out, those red lips of hers surrounding him. She used her tongue so cleverly, to tease him and torment him, the sweetest kind of torment. He bent over her and braced his hands on the counter, felt the cool, smooth granite against his palms and he knew that in seconds he was going to go over.

She seemed to know, too. At the exact last fraction of a second before he was irretrievably lost, she released him, lifted her head and looked up at him.

He said her name, rough and low.

She smiled then, that knowing smile of hers, red lips wet from pleasuring him. And then she put the condom on him, rolling it down with slow, even care, snugging it all the way to the base without once pinching him.

"There," she looked up at him again, pleased with her work. "All ready."

"Come here," he growled the words. "Come up here now."

She rose with catlike grace and he pulled her close, kissing her, spearing his tongue deep, drinking in the heady taste of her. As he kissed her, he eased his hands under that robe of hers, over the lush curves of her hips.

When he had his hands on her bare waist, he lifted her. She knew what to do. She needed no urging. She wrapped those slim, strong legs around him and he was inside.

Nothing. Ever. Had felt as good as that.

His mouth still locked with hers, he turned and tried to brace himself against the counter. It wasn't enough.

She moved on him wildly and he reacted, eagerly keeping rhythm with her. He caught her under her hips, to steady her—and himself. And somehow, he made himself start walking. It was the sweetest agony, every step pushed him deeper into her heat and wetness. She moaned her pleasure into his mouth.

He reeled to the door and turned to lean against it. It worked. He could hold her and move with her and not fear that any second they would crash to the floor.

It was good, so very good. When she came, he felt it acutely, felt her body milking him, drawing the final, glorious explosion of pleasure from him. It sent him over the edge, too. He surged up into her.

She let her head fall back and groaned his name.

And then they sagged there, against the door, panting and laughing, holding on so tight, as the hot tremors of release faded down to a pleasured glow.

She whispered against his throat, "I don't know if I'll ever be able to walk again…"

He kissed her hair. "It's okay. We'll just stay like this. Locked together. Forever…"

"Oh, Luke…" She made a low, sexy sound, fisted a hand in his hair and kissed him.

And then, they just held each other. So tight.

Eventually, with slow care, she unhooked her legs from around his waist and lowered her feet to the floor. She staggered. He steadied her.

"Oh," she sighed soft and low. "Luke Bravo, what you do to me. You only have to touch me and I go up in flames."

Late that night, Mercy lay beside Luke and listened to his breathing even out as he fell asleep. Careful not to wake him, she lifted up on an elbow and studied his face. Even through the thick shadows of the dark room, she could make out the sensual shape of his mouth, the bold jut of his nose.

She wanted to touch him, to trace the line of his strong jaw, to run the pad of her finger along each brow. But she didn't. She only smiled and softly sighed and then lay down again.

He reached for her in his sleep, drawing her close. She let her eyes drift shut, completely content.

She slept through the rest of the night without waking. In the morning, after Luke got up and let the dogs out, he came back to her. She cuddled close to him and they whispered together about how they might spend the day, deciding on a walk around the property and a trip into Fredericksburg.

It was so lovely, every moment of that hot, sunny Saturday. Mercy swore in her heart that, no matter what happened later, she would always treasure this special time they had shared. Holding hands, they strolled the dirt paths that wound through the golden grasses and live oaks near the cabin, the dogs sniffing the ground ahead of them. It was heady, this freedom between them. She felt she could say anything to him, that he would listen and accept her words as honest and heartfelt.

They went to Fredericksburg for lunch. After the meal, they strolled up and down Main Street, stopping in to tour Fort Martin Scott and the Pioneer Museum. They'd left the dogs in the cabin, so they made a point to get back to them by four.

That evening, they sat out on the porch in the blue-painted chairs watching day fade into night. She asked him about his horse breeding program at Bravo Ridge. He spoke of his plans for the ranch with pride, but was modest about his contribution to it.

"I'm an estate manager, really. I love Bravo Ridge and I want to take care of it."

"You do a fine job. All the ranchers I know talk about the horses you raise. You breed so they're suitable for show, but steady-natured. And then you train them to be cow-smart and well-behaved."

His answering smile was almost shy. So strange. Mr. Macho Luke Bravo was really a thoughtful, gentle, caring man.

They spoke again of their families.

"My grandfather was out to create a dynasty," he told her. "He had seven sons."

"And where are your uncles now?"

"Grandpa James chased them away. He was mean and overbearing as they come. But my dad held on. He took what my grandfather left him and he built on it.

BravoCorp is a successful company. We're in land and property development and energy, too. And doing well, even in tough times. Grandpa James made most of his money in oil."

"Which he found on Cabrera land," she reminded him darkly.

"Not until *after* it became Bravo land, and you know it."

"I try not to be bitter." She spoke loftily.

"Good. Where was I?"

"How BravoCorp has made all that money…"

"Right. BravoCorp still makes money in energy. But not only oil now. Wind and solar, too."

"And your father had even more children than your grandfather…."

"Yeah. Seven sons *and* two daughters. My dad's as much into dynasty-building as Grandpa James was. But he's a better man than my grandfather was."

She didn't feel right sitting still for that one. "Come on, Luke. I know about your father. He's famous for being greedy and hardheaded and ambitious."

"And he is. All of the above. I don't deny it. But he's been a good father to all nine of us. He loves us and he loves my mother, deeply. And he shows it. He always made time, when we were kids, to be with us. To pay attention to us. And when faced with the choice between his ambition and what's right for my mom or one of his kids, he'd come down on the side of his children and his wife, every time. He's truehearted, my dad. Even-handed and fair deep down, where it counts."

Was he trying to tell her he thought his father would accept her, if they decided to go forward, to reveal their relationship to their families? She started to ask, but then didn't. It was a beautiful evening and soon they would go inside and make slow, sweet love. That was enough for now. More than enough.

In the trees, the cicadas sang their high, endless song. Luke had lit a mosquito coil, so the bugs left them alone. The dogs snoozed at their feet and the night smelled clean, the air moist as it never was in the heat of the day.

"Nice," she said softly.

He made a low sound of agreement and they turned to each other at the same time. His eyes shone silvery in the gathering dusk. She thought again what a fine-looking man he was. Just the sight of him stole her breath right out of her body.

She said, "I think that's another thing my father resents so deeply. *His* father had only two sons."

Luke grunted. "And one of them died at my grandfather's hand."

"Yes," she agreed with a humorless laugh. "There's that. There's definitely that. But what I also meant is that my dad had one brother, who died. And then, well, he wanted a dynasty, too." She could see in those night-silvered eyes that he remembered what she'd told him yesterday.

He said gently, "But he only had two daughters."

"And only one of us is of his blood—and no, I don't think that means he loves me less. It only means he wanted sons. And more daughters. I think he resented that his enemy, your father, had so many children when he didn't. It was just another way you Bravos were so much richer than we were."

"Was. Were. Past tense. You think maybe he hates us less than he used to?"

"I do, yes. Life is good for him and my mom. It's easier for people to give up their old hatred when their bellies are full and their lives are happy." She sent him a sideways glance. "But he still might not jump up and down for joy if I told him I was wild for you and all you have to do is crook a finger and I come running."

He arched a brow. "Is that true? The part about crooking my finger?"

"Try it."

He did.

With a happy laugh, she rose and went to stand before his chair. "Well?" She lifted her hair off the back of her neck so the night breeze might cool her skin, purposely turning sideways so he could admire the way her breasts lifted with the movement.

He leaned forward in the chair and reached for her, taking her by the waist. She'd worn a gathered, tiered cotton skirt for their trip into town, so it was easy to straddle him, one bare foot dangling to either side of his long, muscular thighs. She rested her arms on his shoulders and bent to brush his lips with a light kiss.

"Strange…" Idly, she stroked his nape with the backs of her fingers.

"What?" He smoothed her full skirt so it covered her knees—and then eased a hand under the light fabric and traced a slow circle on the top of her thigh.

She sighed in pleasure at the caress. "I feel so…easy with you. I am a loyal person, but I don't feel I'm betraying my family when I talk about them to you." She bent close, kissed him again.

"What you tell me, I won't repeat. Ever."

"See, that's the thing. I knew that without you even saying so. But it's nice, to hear you tell it to me out loud."

"I trust you, too, Mercy."

"So then." She slid off his lap and stood gazing down at him, smoothing her skirt. "We have that, no matter what. We have trust."

He rose, too, and wrapped an arm around her, pulling her near. She felt the magic between them, the passion. The heat. "And we have this." His voice was a rough caress. "Tonight. And all day tomorrow. Together."

"Yes, Luke. Oh, yes, we do."

He lowered his head for a slow kiss. When he looked at her again, there was more than sexual desire in his eyes. "I don't want to stop seeing you, after this."

She put two fingers lightly against his lips. "Shh. Kiss me again. Let the future take care of itself…."

Chapter Six

Sunday came too soon.

They made love in the morning light. Mercy memorized every touch, every lingering caress. She would never, ever forget the look in his blue eyes, the way he said her name when he found his release.

And then later, after breakfast, they walked the trails around the cabin again. Luke said that next time they came he would bring a couple of horses and they could ride.

"Next time," she stopped in the dappled shade of an oak. "That sounds promising."

"I told you." His voice was gruff. "I want more."

She bent and picked up a small rock from the path. "Heart-shaped." She held it up for him to see. And then stuck it in her pocket. "A keepsake," she said with a brave smile.

He took her by the shoulders and made her look in those sky-colored eyes. "I want more."

She nodded, slowly. "So do I." And then she let out a long sigh. "But I don't want to be forced to choose, not yet. Do you understand? If we tell the families, there could be trouble. And we would have to make a choice—each other or the people we love."

His grip tightened—not enough to cause her pain, but enough that she knew how strongly he felt. "Maybe there won't be any need for choices, did you think of that? Maybe we're making a big thing out of nothing. So far, you've told Elena and I told Caleb. And both of them said we should go for it."

"Luke. Honestly. Is that what you think your father will say?"

"Damn it, I don't know what my father will say."

"And I don't know what *my* dad will say. I only know that I don't want to hurt him. He doesn't deserve that. I love him so much. And I owe him everything. Without him and Luz I don't know what would have happened to me when my mother got sick. And not only me. What they did for *her*, when she was dying…that was everything. They cared for her, they took her to doctors and then paid the bills. They got the drugs she needed so badly, so she didn't have to die in horrible pain. If right now, today, my dad demanded I stop seeing you…I would do it, Luke. It would be…difficult. So hard. But I would. My honor demands it. Don't you understand?"

His gaze burned into hers. "I do. Of course, I understand."

"But you don't agree?"

"No. I've tried to stay away from you. It didn't work.

And the more thought I give to our little family feud, the more I get what your sister and my brother have been trying to tell us. It's old news, the crap that went down between our families. This, with us…I'm in this now. It's my decision, my life. My family has to understand that. I honor them. I love them. But they don't get to decide who I'm going to be with."

She pulled free of his grip and turned away to look out over the rolling land, at the golden grasses and the wide, blue sky above. Several feet ahead, the dogs had flopped down on the trail. They panted happily, their pink tongues lolling, waiting for a signal to get moving again.

"It's different for you." She spoke without turning, letting the hot summer wind carry her words back to him. "You were born into your family. They are your blood. You owe them your life, yes, and a son's loyalty. And I don't belittle that. But I owe Luz and Javier even more."

"So much that you'll lie and sneak around to be with me?" His voice from behind her held a bitter edge. "Where's the honor in that?"

She made herself face him then, and she tipped her chin high. The wind blew her hair across her mouth. She shoved the strands out of the way. "We don't have to lie or sneak around. We just don't have to tell them that we're together. San Antonio is a big city. We don't have to hide. We just…don't have to make a big announcement."

"A lie by omission, you mean."

It was right, what he said. And Mercy didn't deny it. "Yes. A lie by omission. That's what I want. So we can have more time together. Before the choice comes."

His eyes were narrowed—with anger? With disgust

for her cowardice? She didn't know. He asked, "And when the choice does come—*if* it comes—what then?"

She answered honestly. "Luke. I don't know. My dad lost his father and his only brother in battling your family. My dad lost his family home, La Joya, that you now call Bravo Ridge."

"And we lost nothing, is that what you're saying?"

She didn't waver. "That's right. Nothing. Nothing that I can see. You Bravos gained at our expense."

"My grandfather may have been one mean SOB, but he won Bravo Ridge fair and square. It was an accident that killed your grandfather. And your uncle died trying to kill my grandfather. My grandfather was wounded in that confrontation—gutshot. He was lucky to survive."

"I know how the story goes. But nothing changes the facts. Two men in my family are dead and no one died in your family. It doesn't change what happened when my mother went to work for your father. However well-meaning your father was to hire her, the end result was the near-destruction of her marriage and yet more bitterness between our families."

A long moment of tense silence elapsed before he spoke. "You said last night that you thought your father was getting over his hatred of my family."

"I did. And I do think that. But Luke, I'm just not ready to put him to the test."

He was silent again. The sun was bright and hot overhead, but to Mercy, the day seemed darker somehow. "So that's it, then, those are the options?" he asked at last. "We sneak around, or it's over."

She resisted the urge to correct him, to tell him again

that they wouldn't be sneaking around, they would just be keeping their relationship to themselves. In the end, it didn't matter what name you gave it. She wasn't ready yet to tell her father that she was seeing a Bravo, a Bravo who made her burn with just a touch.

"Yes," she answered quietly. "That's it. We keep what we have to ourselves for a while. That's all I'm asking. Will you please just consider it?"

His jaw was set. "It's not my style."

"I know, but if we could only—"

He cut her off. "Mercy. I'm telling you that sneaking around isn't going to work for me. If you won't change your mind about it, I don't want to take this thing between us any further."

His words pierced her like a knife. Yet, somehow, she held her ground. She gave a slow nod. "I hate it, but I get it."

He looked at her long and hard. The few feet of distance between them yawned like a canyon a thousand miles wide. Finally, he swore low. "We should get back."

"Yes. All right."

He turned and started toward the cabin. She followed behind him, the dogs at her heels, her heart aching as if it was breaking in two. Somehow, in her determination to put off the moment when she would have to choose, she had ended up making a choice, after all.

She was losing Luke. Losing him when she'd only just found him. How could that be? And how could it hurt so much?

He was right, though, she told herself. Honor mattered. It bound them both. Better to stand up proudly and face their families—or end it now. Her heart ached, but she would get over it. The longer they were together, the harder it would be to heal if it ended badly.

And all because I am a coward.

Luke had been kind. He'd never called her a coward straight out. Not in so many words. But she knew he thought it.

Yet, still, who could say how long this thing between them might last if they kept on? It didn't feel possible that she could ever stop wanting him.

But it could happen. Their passion could wear itself out, the way her relationship with Jack had. Just slowly fade from flame to ember. And from there, to cool ash.

Was that what she had wanted, really, if she had been brutally honest with him? To keep what they shared a secret until it had time to die, to slowly fade away?

He was right, she told herself yet again as she entered the cabin in his wake. He was right and she knew it. They were ending it today and it was the wise choice. Eventually, she would get over him. Life was like that. Broken hearts healed and you moved on. She would get over him and she would have the memory of this beautiful weekend, always....

They packed up their suitcases in silence and loaded the pickup. The drive to San Antonio seemed to take centuries. They didn't speak a word to each other the whole way. By why should they? There was nothing more to say.

Her pickup was waiting where she'd left it in the clinic parking lot. Luke got her suitcase for her and put it in the back. She helped Orlando up to his seat and got in behind the wheel. Luke came and shut her door for her.

She started up the engine and rolled down the window. "I had such a beautiful time. I'll never forget it. Thank you."

He swallowed. Hard. And nodded.

"Goodbye," she said.

He gripped the open window frame with both hands, tight. But only for a moment. Then he slapped the door with his palms and stepped back.

The tears were rising. She blinked them down furiously. She had no right to cry. She had made this choice and she would live by it. Careful not to glance at him as he stood watching her leave, she backed from the space and drove away.

Chapter Seven

"So how was your weekend, *mija?*" her mother asked on Monday night when Mercy joined the family for dinner at the beautiful Mediterranean-style house her dad had built seven years ago.

"I had a wonderful time," she said, as Elena, seated across the table, caught her eye. The dimple in Elena's cheek warned that she was barely holding back a knowing grin. Mercy tried to telegraph her a threatening look without giving herself away. Elena responded by fluttering her eyelashes, that telltale dimple deepening.

"Who did you go with?" Luz frowned, apparently oblivious to the glances flying back and forth between her daughters. "You were about to tell me Thursday, weren't you? But I had to take that other call...."

While Mercy tried frantically to decide how to answer, her dad said, "You work too much, *mi amore.*"

Her mother beamed a loving smile at Javier. "*Es verdad.* But it's hard times for so many. We're fortunate to do well." She cast a satisfied glance around the dining room with its graceful arched doorways and heavily carved mahogany and mesquite furniture. "And that means, always, hard work." Mercy dared to hope that the dangerous question had been left behind—but no such luck. "So?" Her mother turned a fond glance on her again. "Who did you go with?"

Mercy cleared her throat. "Um, I…"

"Olympia and Jocasta, didn't you say?" Elena cut in cheerfully. Mercy sent her sister a dirty look, but Elena only gazed back calmly, golden-brown eyes wide and innocent. "They're Greek. I can hardly pronounce their last name. Kal-o-yer-o-pou-lis." Elena made a big production of sounding out the made-up name of Mercy's nonexistent friends. "Right, Mercy?"

"Do I know them?" asked Luz. She turned again to their father, still frowning. "Should I know them?" Javier shrugged. And Luz asked Mercy again, "Have I met them?"

And again, Elena answered for her. "I don't think so, Mom." She had the gall to look thoughtful. "Mercy met them at A&M, remember? Olympia was studying landscape architecture. And Jocasta was getting a degree in finance. They're twins, but not identicals. And they've got that cabin up in the Hill Country. They were always saying they would have to take Mercy up there one of these days. And now they finally have."

Javier said, "That was nice of them."

"Mmm-hmm," said Mercy, and ate another bite of

delicious cilantro-flavored carne asada. Her mother was not only a successful realtor, she was an amazing cook.

"So what did you do up there all weekend?" Elena asked with another of those thoroughly annoying oh so innocent expressions.

Mercy had to resist the urge to kick her sister under the table. "We hiked some really beautiful trails. And we went into Fredericksburg to visit the Pioneer Museum."

"So nice to get away," murmured Elena much too passionately. "And breathe that fresh country air…"

Their dad asked, "How are things at the veterinary clinic?"

Mercy could have kissed him. And not only for changing the subject. He was a good man, her dad. And so handsome—not tall, but powerfully built, with soft brown eyes and black hair just beginning to turn silver at the temples.

"Going great," she said. "I'm mostly in the field." When you worked with large animals, you went to them. Mercy loved spending her days outdoors. "Doc Brewer says when he comes back, we'll keep it that way. He'll stick with the clinic and I'll take the calls."

"You're happy, then, with your job?" Javier asked.

"I am, Dad. Very happy."

"Good. Work, love, family." He winked at Luz. "What else is there, eh?"

After dinner, Elena led the way upstairs.

When they reached her room, she ushered Mercy in first. As soon as they were both past the threshold, Elena shut and locked the door. She pretended to sag against it. "I love them with all my heart. You know that. But my condo will be ready October fifteenth and I can't wait."

Mercy only folded her arms across her chest and glared.

Elena lifted her thick hair off the back of her neck. "Oh, go ahead. Say it."

"You know that lying is a sin."

"Somebody had to step up." Elena gathered her hair in her fist and twisted it in a knot at the crown of her head. She took a long pin from a tray on the dresser and eased it in place. "You were out of your depth and sinking fast."

Mercy went to the window and gazed out over the backyard. Last year, their dad had put in a pool. It was beautiful, a freeform lagoon style, with varicolored tile and a fountain, tall grasses and green ferns. "Well. You won't have to lie for me again. It's over."

Elena let out cry. "What do you mean over? It just got started."

"It didn't work out."

"But you're crazy for him."

"I really don't want to go into it." Mercy stared down at the sparkling fountain, refusing to turn and meet her sister's eyes.

But Elena wouldn't stand for that. She took her shoulders and guided her around. "*Chica,* don't cry…" Elena pulled her close.

Mercy didn't resist. It was all an act, trying to be strong. She needed the comfort. "I think maybe I love him, Elena." She whispered the awful truth, holding on tight. "But how can that be possible? All we had was a weekend together."

"Sometimes that's all it takes." Elena stroked her hair.

"Love's not always careful and slow. Sometimes it's like a bolt of lightning, swift and bright and oh so hot."

Mercy laughed through her tears and pulled away enough to capture her sister's face between her hands. "Where did you learn so much about love?"

"Some women are born wise," said Elena in a lofty tone.

Mercy let her hands drop to her sides. "Well, I've lost him now. Even if it really was love, I need to learn to get over him."

Elena swore low in Spanish. "*¿Por qué?* Did he dump you?"

"No. No, he never…"

"Well, then, what happened?"

"I wanted to keep the thing between us secret for a while. He wouldn't do that."

Elena made a low sound. "I love you, Mercy mine. But you are a fool if you let that man go. Didn't you hear yourself? You just said you love him."

"I said I *think* I love him…."

"Mercy, you're smarter than that. You're braver than that. You can't let some old family problem get between you and happiness. Go to him. Tell him you were wrong—which you were. Tell him you will be proud to stand up with him as his woman, that you're not letting your pointless, stupid fears hold you back."

Mercy tried to drum up a little outrage. "My fears are not stupid."

Elena wasn't impressed. "Oh, yes. They are. They're stupid and you have to get past them."

Mercy glanced toward the shut door to the hall and lowered her voice. "I can't bear to hurt them."

"Are you kidding?" Elena took the hint and brought the volume down, too. "They'll be fine. Give them a little credit, why don't you?"

Mercy realized she'd needed so badly to hear exactly what her sister was telling her now. "You think so?"

"I'm certain."

"Should I talk to them first, maybe? See if they—"

"Mercy. Do you want to be with him or not?"

"Oh, I do. Yes, yes, I do."

"Then first things first. Go to him. Ask for another chance."

"What if he—?"

Elena put up a hand. "Stop second-guessing. Just go. Just tell him you want to try again."

Tell him you want to try again....

Elena's advice stuck with her.

Not that she worked up the nerve to do the necessary follow-through. That night, when she got home, she picked up the phone and dialed the first two digits of the number at the ranch. And then she hesitated.

And that did it. She slammed the phone down, her courage fled.

Maybe, she started thinking, she ought to wait a few days. Maybe she was blowing her feelings for Luke out of proportion. Maybe, with a little time, the yearning— for his touch, his kiss, the rough, low sound of his voice—would diminish.

She decided to wait a little while. To see if the longing to be with him lessened.

It didn't. Not on Tuesday. Or Thursday. Not on Friday or Saturday or Sunday, either.

She went to mass with the family—after a quick trip to confession the night before. Elena kept shooting her questioning looks. Mercy was careful not to let their glances collide. She knelt in the pew and kept her head humbly bowed. When Father Francis called them to communion, Mercy filed up to the altar with the rest of the family.

She hugged them all outside the church and said she had to get back to the clinic for a while so she wouldn't be able to come home for the Sunday meal.

Elena called her on Monday afternoon. "You didn't take my advice, did you?"

"I love you, Elena, but it's my life, you know?"

Elena sighed. "You're right. I give up. I will say no more. You can stop avoiding me."

Mercy laughed. "Good. Because I miss you, baby sister."

So Elena came over. They did mani-pedis, made popcorn, watched a romantic comedy. Luke's name was not mentioned.

Elena left at a little after eleven. Mercy saw her to the door and then she picked up the phone and called Bravo Ridge.

It rang several times. Finally a woman answered— groggy voiced, with a slight Spanish accent. "Bravo Ridge Ranch. Zita speaking."

Mercy almost hung up. But she was tired of her own cowardice, just sick to death of it. She stayed on the line—and started apologizing in Spanish. *"Lo siento que es tan tarde…"* Get a grip, damn it. She sucked in a breath and said what she wanted. "Luke Bravo, please."

"Un momento. I will see if he is still awake…." A clicking sound.

And then silence. Mercy waited. For several seconds that seemed like hours.

Finally, another click. "This is Luke."

Ah, Dios. Just the sound of his voice made a hollow feeling in the pit of her stomach, made her knees feel weak and her heart pound as if it would burst through the walls of her chest.

"Hello? Who's there?"

She made herself speak. "Um. Hi. It's—"

He knew her voice. "Mercy."

What to say? How to tell him. "I, well, I was wondering...I was..."

"Are you all right? Is there something—?"

"No. Fine. Really. I'm fine."

He blew out a breath. "Whew. Okay, then."

"Luke, I keep, well, I can't stop thinking. Can't stop wondering if maybe we..." The words ran out. And her throat had clutched up. She swallowed. Hard.

"Yeah?" He sounded...hopeful. Didn't he?

She coughed to loosen the awful constricted feeling. "If I said I would be braver. If I said we didn't have to hide..."

"Mercy."

"Um. Yeah?"

"Are you at your house?"

"Yeah. I am. I'm at home."

"Stay there."

"But Luke—"

"Don't even move. I'm on my way."

Chapter Eight

Luke couldn't believe she'd called him first.

It had been a week and two days since he left her in front of the clinic. Every day—every hour—he'd had to stop himself from reaching for the phone.

From capitulating to her demand that they lie and sneak around to be together.

He had been weakening. There was just…something about her. Something that got to him the way no other woman ever had. He'd know that he wouldn't last much longer. Within a day or two, he would have thrown his pride to the wind and begged her to give him another chance. On her terms. In her way. However she wanted it, he would agree.

But compromising his principles to be near her wouldn't be necessary now. *She* had called *him*. He parked in front of her house and strode boldly up her front walk.

Just like that time before, she was waiting for him. She pulled open the door.

He went in.

She shut the door.

That three-legged dog of hers wiggled over. "Hey, there, Orlando." Luke bent and greeted him.

When he rose to his feet again, she stood maybe two feet away. He drank in the sight of her, her midnight hair loose on her shoulders, those dark eyes so wide and full of wanting, her body, in that little white wisp of a robe she'd worn at the cabin, yearning toward him.

"Oh, Luke…"

He reached for her and hauled her close, scenting flowers and exotic spice, feeling her heat and womanly softness. The kiss they shared set the night on fire.

When he lifted his head, he cupped her beautiful face in his two cherishing hands. His feeling of triumph at winning their standoff had vanished. He only wanted to get straight with her, to reveal himself in ways he would never, before her, have imagined he could do. "I'm so damn glad you called. I wouldn't have lasted much longer."

"You mean that?" She gazed up at him, her sweet face flushed with happiness.

He nodded. "What is it you do to me, Mercy?"

She let out a shaky, excited breath. "Oh, I don't know. I don't understand it, either. But it's…pretty amazing, huh?"

"And scary."

A laugh trembled through her. "Yeah. That, too."

He brushed another kiss across her lips. She sighed and leaned closer. He wanted to scoop her up and take her to bed right then. But he had more he needed to say. "I did think about the things you told me Sunday up at the cabin. About how, in all this mess with our two families, the Cabreras *have* suffered more than us Bravos. About how it's harder for you than for me. With what Luz and Javier did for you and your mother, with how they saved you, gave you love and support, made you one of their own when they didn't have to…I see now, Mercy. I get it. I do."

She pressed her lips together and shook her head. "But I know what you were thinking that day. And you were right. I *am* a coward…"

Tenderly, he stroked her shining hair, marveling at the fact that he was here with her again. At last. He admitted, "I did think you were cowardly. And I was wrong. You don't want to hurt them if you can help it, not after all they've done for you. You love them too much. You're a good daughter—a woman who puts others ahead of herself—not a coward at all."

Moisture shimmered in her eyes. "I think you do understand." He touched her velvety cheek, brushing away a tear with his thumb. She whispered, "Please, Luke. Kiss me now. Love me now…"

She didn't have to ask twice. He lowered his head and he kissed her, long and thoroughly. And then he scooped her high against his chest and commanded in a rough whisper, "Your bedroom."

She tucked her head under his chin and pointed the way.

He carried her down a short hallway into a room with walls the color of sunflowers and a red comforter on the bed. She'd left the nightstand lamp on. In its soft glow, he set her down on the red rug beside the bed and untied the sash of her robe. He dropped the bit of silk to the rug and then eased the robe off her shoulders. It fell away, light as a cloud.

But when he urged her down onto the bed, she resisted. She kissed him and she reached for his belt buckle, smiling softly against his lips as she unbuckled it.

He surrendered, standing patiently before her as she took away his belt and his shirt. She walked him backward and pushed him into a padded chair in the corner. Then she knelt and took his Wranglers all the way down. She pulled off his boots and his socks. He watched her, admiring the sleek beauty of her naked body, the blue-black shine to her hair and the olive luster of her bare skin, as she finished undressing him.

When he was naked, she rose up to her knees. He held out a hand. When she took it, he opened his thighs and pulled her against him, so she rested with her head on his bare chest.

He stroked her hair, ran a finger down the bumps of her spine. "It hurt me," he whispered against her silky hair, "to miss you that much."

She turned her head, her hair like a froth of silk against his flesh. She pressed her lips to the center of his chest, breathed, "I know. Oh, Luke, I know…" against his skin. She scraped her teeth there, where her lips had been. And then licked him, a long, wet stroke of her tongue. "I missed everything, the sound of your voice, your sky-pale eyes, the feel of you, and the taste…."

He hooked her chin with a finger and guided her face up to him. She rose higher on her knees, until her sweet lips met his.

As he kissed her, he stroked a hand down between

their bodies, lingering on the full curve of a breast. She gasped as he rolled her nipple between his thumb and forefinger. And then he moved lower.

He found the springy curls at the apex of her thighs, eased a finger in and down, lower still. At last, he felt the heart of her womanhood. He parted her. She moaned into his mouth.

She was wet and so silky. He stroked the soft, slick folds. She groaned and worked her hips against his hand, eager. Open for him.

He wanted to be inside her. He *needed* that. Needed the hot feel of her slickness claiming him.

After that mess up at the cabin, the necessity for protection was burned into his brain. Even in the heat of his desire for her, he remembered this time. He muttered the question against her mouth.

"Yes," she answered on a low moan. She caught his lip between her teeth, tugging lightly, before she let go. "In the drawer by the bed...."

It wasn't that far away. And the softness of the bed would be welcome, anyway. He took her by the waist and rose. She went with him, her lips pressed to his as they stood.

Three steps and they were by the bed. Never breaking the kiss, she reached for the drawer. Clever girl, she had a condom out of the box in seconds. She pushed the drawer shut.

And she did break their kiss as she tore open the pouch. She had it free instantly and she rolled it down over him. Then she glanced up at him, eyes soft and so willing.

That time, when he urged her onto the bed, she didn't resist. She lay down among the red pillows. He came down on top of her, too eager to take it slowly. Sliding his knee between her smooth thighs, he settled himself against her. She opened for him, reaching down between them to put him in just the right spot.

He pushed in. Her body welcomed him, soft and sweet and very hot.

She wrapped her arms and legs around him. "Oh, Luke. Yes. Like that…" She rose to meet him.

He breathed her name against her throat. "Mine," he heard himself whisper, lost in her. Never wanting to be found. "Mine…"

"Always," she told him as she rose and fell beneath him. *"Siempre. Hasta el fin de tiempo."* She caught his face in her hands and she sought his eyes. "Whenever, wherever. Whatever happens, even if we don't end up together, deep in my heart, Luke, I will be yours.…"

In time, they slept, naked, their arms and legs tangled together, not needing a blanket in the early-September heat.

Mercy woke to the soft drone of the window air conditioner. The lamp by the bed was still on and Luke wasn't with her. She sat up with a disappointed cry.

"It's okay. I'm here." He sat, fully dressed, in the corner chair. She saw a gentle smile curve his lips. "I was watching you sleep. You look like an angel. So peaceful and sweet. I thought about what it's like to make love with you, to hold you in my arms. I thought that, whatever happens, I'm a very lucky man."

She smiled in pleasure at his words and pushed her tangled hair from her eyes. "You're dressed. You're leaving?"

He nodded. "Soon. It's after three."

"The night goes too fast when I have you with me." She bent over the edge of the bed and found her robe waiting in a silky puddle, the sash beside it. Scooping it up, she wrapped it around her.

He waited, watching, his eyes gleaming through the shadows. Once she'd knotted the sash, he said, "I've been thinking…"

"Tell me." Her hair was caught under the robe's collar. She lifted it free. "What?"

"I've never been one to compromise on what I believe is right. I don't want to sneak around to be with you."

"I know. I understand. We discussed this already. And I'm willing to—"

He put up a hand. "Let me finish." At her nod, he continued, "What I'm thinking is that you're right, too. Both of us are. I don't want to lie about being with you. And you don't want to hurt the ones you love the most."

What a fine man he was, truly. Thoughtful. And good to the core. "Yes. That's right."

The corner of his mouth quirked in the start of a smile. "We're both adults. There's no reason we have to ask our families for their permission to be together. I'm not willing to sneak around. But I am willing, for a while anyway, to just…not say anything to anyone, the way you suggested that last day at the cabin. If you come to me at Bravo Ridge, you come openly. When I'm here at your house, my pickup will be parked out in front for any passerby to see. If we go out to dinner or catch a movie, we go proudly, with our heads high. Maybe someone in one of our families will figure it out. If that happens, I want openness.

We face any questions squarely and we deal with them honestly. We don't lie. Will that work for you?"

"For a while, you mean?"

"Yeah. A few weeks. A month. Until it ends between us. Or until we agree we both want more."

More. She took his meaning, saw it crystal clear. More: as in forever. As in wedding bells and gold rings and the simple, earth-shattering words, *I love you.*

As for it ending, every day that passed, as her longing and the depth of her feeling for him grew, an ending seemed all the more impossible. But the future, after all, was a mystery. Full of strange twists and turns. Anything might happen. Her heart denied that, but in her mind, she knew it for the truth.

"Well?" he asked.

She slid off the bed and paused on the red rug to tuck the sides of the robe more securely in place. "Yes. It's a good compromise. Thank you for seeing my side of it."

He rose, took her shoulders and kissed her, a hard kiss, one that was much too brief. "Tonight…"

"I'm working at least till six."

"Come to me at Bravo Ridge when you finish."

"Yes. Oh, yes, I'll be there."

For Mercy, the September days that followed passed in a haze of pure happiness.

They were together almost every night at Mercy's house or at Bravo Ridge. Those nights were heaven. Mercy lived for the touch of his lips on hers, the scent of him on her sheets….

That first Friday night after they got back together,

they went out to dinner and then to a movie. While they were in line to buy the movie tickets, Luke spotted an old friend from high school. He introduced the guy to Mercy. She smiled and said she was pleased to meet him.

And that was that. No repercussions.

No one in either of the families suspected a thing—or if they did, no one asked.

Even Elena, who had begun her first job as a middle-school teacher, said nothing. She had agreed to leave the subject of Luke alone, and she kept her word. Mercy wondered if her sister knew that she and Luke were back together. But she decided not to ask. Better to leave Elena out of it. Mercy and Luke had made their decision as to how they would handle their love affair. She didn't need Elena on the case, telling her what she *should* be doing, urging her to have it out with Javier and Luz.

Luke took her to the cabin in the Hill Country again the next weekend. He towed a horse trailer behind the big extended cab pickup and instead of walking the trails on the property, they rode on horseback. For Orlando, he even brought a special seat he'd found in a feed store. Since the dog couldn't keep up, he rode in front of Mercy's saddle, tongue hanging out with pleasure to be taken along.

Saturday, they packed a picnic lunch and spread a blanket under the shade of an oak. The horses grazed contentedly and the dogs sprawled in the grass and Mercy and Luke made love right out there in the wide open.

When they headed for home Sunday afternoon, she wished they didn't have to go. She could have stayed at the cabin forever, just the two of them and the dogs and the horses.

Monday night, Mercy had dinner at her parents' house. And Tuesday, Luke came to her at her place.

After they made love, as they lay naked on her bed, the sweat drying on their bodies, he told her that Thursday night, his mom was planning a family party at the ranch in honor of Mary Bravo's twenty-ninth birthday. Mary and Gabe, Luke's older brother, had been married in Lake Tahoe just two months before.

"It's a way to welcome Mary to the family," he said. "And you're invited."

Alarm jangled through her. "You mean you've told your family about us?"

He laughed and kissed the tip of her nose. "Uh-uh. But I will if you say yes."

"Oh, Luke…"

"I'll take that as a no." He rolled to his back and put an arm over his eyes.

She canted up on an elbow and hesitantly touched the curved, upturned fingers of his hand. "You're angry."

He lowered his arm and met her eyes. "No. Just disappointed. But I'll live." He accepted her kiss when she bent close.

"It's too soon."

"It's all right."

"And springing me on your family at your sister-in-law's birthday party…"

He made a low sound in his throat. "I see where you're going. Bad idea, huh?"

She kissed him again. "Well, when and if it happens, I don't think it should be at someone else's party."

"Yes, ma'am."

She rested her head on his hard chest, and listened

contentedly to the steady beat of his heart. "I don't think I've ever been this happy…."

He touched her hair, stroking. "I know what you mean. I feel the same."

That Thursday night, the formal dining room at Bravo Ridge was filled with family talk and laughter. Davis and Aleta Bravo sat at either end of the table and beamed in pride at each other. All nine of their children had managed to be there for the party.

Mary Hofstetter Bravo glowed with happiness and said she was so pleased to be part of the family. She had a doting Gabe on one side and her mother-in-law from her first marriage, Ida Hofstetter, on the other. The baby, Ginny, born on the day Mary and Gabe met, sat in a high chair between husband and wife making happy baby noises and occasionally banging her plastic spoon on the high chair tray. Gabe doted on that kid. He clearly adored Mary. And he also really seemed to like Ida, who had a no-nonsense attitude and a thoughtful look in her eye.

Luke watched the new family, envying them a little. They made him think of Mercy, made him want things he knew damn well he might never get: the simple pleasure of having her at his side during family dinners like this one. The chance to share an intimate glance while the others spoke of mundane things.

Ash, the oldest of Luke's brothers, sat halfway down the table, his wife Tessa at his side. The two of them looked as happy as Mary and Gabe—if that was possible. Once, when Davis raised his glass in a toast to the birthday girl, Ash bent close to his wife and they shared a quick, fond kiss. The sight made Luke's chest feel tight. At that moment, seeing his brothers' happiness so openly displayed for all to see, he resented his family. If he hadn't been born a Bravo, Mercy wouldn't want to keep herself separate from the rest of his life. She would be sitting next to him tonight.

The situation depressed him. He had more wine than he should have. And two brandies with the birthday cake.

When the party was over, everyone went home except Davis and Aleta, who decided to stay the night. Luke didn't feel much like sleeping, so he went to his office at the back of the house. He poured himself a whiskey and dropped into the swivel chair at his desk.

Hoisting his booted feet up on the desktop, he sipped his drink and considered going to Mercy. He wanted to wrap himself in her warmth and softness, to lose himself in the tempting scent of her skin. When he was with her, the building frustration he felt with their agreement to not tell their families didn't eat at him as much. When he looked in her black eyes, he knew she belonged to him and nothing else really mattered.

But no. He wouldn't go to her. It was way too late. Let her have her sleep for once. Since they'd gotten back together, he'd been keeping her up every night, making love and then talking to all hours. Besides, he'd had too much to drink to be getting behind the wheel of a car.

The soft tap at the door surprised him. He'd thought everyone was asleep.

"It's open."

The door swung inward. It was his dad, dressed for

bed in dark silk pajamas and a robe to match. "Mind if I join you?"

Luke nodded at the liquor cart against the wall and watched Davis as he poured himself a drink. At fifty-eight, his dad remained a good-looking man. Davis was tall and fit. His hair had turned silver, but he still had a full head of it.

Davis took the club chair near the desk. He sipped his whiskey. "Good party."

Luke raised his glass. "Mom did a great job, as always."

"You weren't real talkative tonight." Beneath still-dark brows, his ice-green eyes were watchful.

Luke grunted. He'd never been a big talker at family gatherings. "That's news?"

His father stared down at the whiskey in his glass, as if the answer to some important question lurked there. Then the green eyes zeroed in on Luke again. "You got something on your mind, son?"

Luke studied his father's face. "Maybe I should be asking you that question."

Davis knocked back another slug of booze, wincing as it burned a hot trail down his throat. And then came out with it. "Word is you're seeing a gorgeous Latina. You're seeing her often."

So. This was it. They were outed. Mercy wouldn't be happy, but too bad. The rules were that he would lie only by omission. Direct questions would be answered truthfully. "Word from who?"

His father shook his head. "Luke. You've taken her to the cabin twice. She comes here two or three nights a week and the other nights, you're out, presumably with her."

Luke repeated, "Word from who?"

His father heaved a weary sigh. "You were seen out together a couple of weeks ago by a colleague of mine. He mentioned it to me."

"Who?"

"What does it matter?"

"I'll ask again. Who?"

"Logan Tallent."

Luke vaguely recognized the name. "I hardly know the man."

"What did you expect?"

"I expected Logan Tallent and everyone else to mind their own damn business."

His father shook his head. "Don't be naive. People know that there's bad blood between us and the Cabreras. If one of us is seen with one of them, people notice."

"So Logan Tallent came running to you with the big news that he'd seen your son out with a Cabrera. And then you started spying on me."

"I've been asking questions and demanding answers of the people in my employ."

"Poor Zita. She's seemed kind of freaky lately. You must have scared her to death. And the Hoffmans." The Hoffmans took care of the cabin in the Hill Country. "Did you threaten to fire them if they didn't report back to you with all the juicy details of when I was at the cabin, who was with me and what we did while we were there?"

"Nobody's getting fired. I asked them to tell me what was going on and they did. And then I stayed out of it, minded my own business, hoping it would end quickly without any intervention. But it doesn't seem to be ending."

Luke stared at his father levelly. "No. It's not ending." He thought of his mother, at dinner, looking so proud and happy to have the whole family together. "Does Mom know about this, too?"

His dad glanced away. "I decided it was better to leave her out of it."

"But I thought the two of you believed in total honesty with each other."

"There's no reason to get her all upset over this."

"How do you know she would be upset? Maybe she would surprise you, Dad."

"I think, for now at least, we can just discuss this, man-to-man."

"For that, I'm going to need another drink." Luke swung his boots to the floor and went to the liquor cart.

His father watched him pour the amber liquid from the crystal decanter. "Is it serious?"

Luke put the stopper back in the decanter and returned to the desk. He dropped into his chair. "Yeah. It's serious."

"Do Luz and Javier know?"

Luke set his glass down on the desk blotter. "No. Mercy doesn't want them to know. She can't stand for what we have together to stir up old animosities. I wanted her to come to the party tonight. She refused."

"A wise decision on her part."

Luke picked up his glass again. But instead of drinking from it, he set it back down—hard. Booze sloshed onto his hand. He licked it off. "As far as I'm concerned, Dad, this war between her family and ours is nothing but bull—"

"You don't know what you're talking about." Davis cut in before he could finish. "Her father hates us. All of us. You included. You're a Bravo and that makes you the enemy. If you care about her—and about your own family—you'll end it with her."

The irony was he would probably lose her anyway, now. Once she knew that Davis knew, the moment he'd been dreading would come. She would have to make a choice.

Luke had a very strong feeling that the choice wouldn't go in his favor. "Go to bed, Dad."

Davis rose. He set his glass on the edge of the desk. "You think I don't wish it could be different? In my day, I tried to bridge the gap. To end the war that started when your grandfather won that horserace and claimed this land for our family. But it's…what it is, between them and us. It's better to accept it. Stay clear of them. Whenever we get mixed up with them, it always ends in trouble."

"It's crap, Dad. Just old noise."

"Give her up, son. Find someone else."

"It's none of your business. Stay out of it. Stop making Zita and the Hoffmans spy for you. It's beneath you."

"If you would only listen to—"

Luke threw his drink. It shattered against the far wall. Booze and broken glass rained down. Quietly, for the second time, he said, "Go to bed, Dad."

Finally, Davis turned and left him.

Chapter Nine

Mercy woke Friday morning missing Luke. She smiled at her own neediness. He'd come to her Wednesday night. She would see him after work tonight. Really, she had to get over this hunger to be with him every minute of every day.

She almost called him before she left for the clinic, just to hear his voice. But she told herself she was being silly. Tonight would be soon enough. She would go to him at Bravo Ridge, as they had agreed when he left her bed Thursday morning before dawn.

First thing at the clinic, she got a call on a sick calf. She headed for a small ranch near Castroville.

She'd just finished a successful surgery to remove a roll of bailing twine the calf had swallowed, when her mother called and invited her to lunch. Mercy rubbed the calf blood off her watch and checked the time. It was ten to eleven.

"I'll need to clean up a little. Would one be okay?"

"Yes. One. That's fine." Luz sounded anxious.

"Mom? Is everything all right?"

"Yes. Of course. A crazy day…" She named a place they both liked in El Mercado—Market Square, downtown. "See you there…"

After Mercy hung up, she told the rancher what to watch for as the calf convalesced and promised to be back in a week to see how the little one was doing. Then she drove home for a shower and a change of clothes.

Her mom was already there, holding a table for them, when Mercy joined her at the restaurant. They ordered fajitas and a pair of tall iced teas and ate too many tortilla chips *con queso,* talking of inconsequential things while they waited for the main dish to come.

Luz wore a slim black skirt and a fitted turquoise silk blouse, her hair pulled back in a sophisticated twist, the pearls Javier had given her for their twenty-fifth anniversary complementing the dusky color of her smooth, youthful skin. Mercy marveled at her mother sometimes. Luz thrived on working long hours. She was almost fifty, but she looked thirty-five. Clients would call her before dawn or long after dark, wanting to see this or that house, needing to be reassured that the house they had just signed a contract on was really right for them. Luz never skipped a call or a chance to make a sale. She was dedicated to her work and her clients and, above all, the prosperity of her family.

Mercy leaned across the table. "You're looking *muy bonita,* Mom."

Luz smiled softly at the compliment and smoothed her sleek hair. "Ah, *mija*. But the years do go by...."

Mercy thought of Luke then—for no reason other than that lately, she was always thinking of him. Random images of him would pop into her head often during the day. She could see him in her mind's eye, as he had looked before dawn yesterday morning, blue eyes lazy after lovemaking.

Funny how the world seemed more vivid, Mercy thought, more beautiful, when a woman had a special man—a man whose touch could set her body on fire. A good man with a true heart. A man she could be quiet with. Or talk with all night long.

She beamed at her mom.

Luz gazed back at her steadily, not smiling anymore. Wistfully, she murmured, "You look so happy, *mija*."

Mercy frowned. Something in her mother's expression wasn't right. Was there some kind of trouble? "Mom. Is something wrong?"

Before Luz could answer, the waiter came with their still-sizzling lunch of spicy beef and peppers and onions. He flipped out a serving tray and put everything on it, transferring the food to the table from there.

"*Mucho caliente*," the waiter warned them with a wink. The hot steel plates were set on wooden chargers. He slid the chargers in front of them. Then came the lidded ceramic bowls containing warm tortillas. "*Mas* chips?"

"No, *gracias*." Her mother granted him a distracted smile. He refilled their iced tea glasses and left them.

Mercy began loading up a couple of tortillas with fajita meat and vegetables, spreading on a little hot salsa, guacamole and sour cream before rolling the tortilla up into a burrito. She took a bite. A big one. "Mmm…" She savored the flavors. But when she swallowed and looked across at her mother, Luz was just sitting there. She hadn't touched the tempting food. Mercy set down her fajita. "Okay, Mom. Something's wrong. Please tell me what."

Luz nudged her charger away a little and folded her hands on the table. She leaned toward Mercy and spoke so softly that Mercy had to lean in, too, just to hear her over the babble of voices in the busy restaurant. "I don't…know how to say this." She muttered something low in Spanish. "I don't even know where to begin…."

Mercy's stomach lurched. It must be something really bad. She pushed her own charger away, her appetite fled. "What? *Dígame.* You're scaring me."

Luz fingered the triple strand of pearls at her throat, as if she would draw comfort from them. Like the beads of a rosary, her slim fingers ticked them off. She closed her eyes, whispered in Spanish. Something about it being all her fault.

Mercy reached across and caught her mother's hand. *"Mami, por favor…"*

Luz gave her fingers a squeeze and then released them. "I…got a call from a friend this morning."

Mercy's heart pounded in a sick, frantic way. "What friend?"

Luz waved the question away. "It doesn't matter who. It matters what my friend told me. You've been seen, often, with one of the Bravo sons."

Seen, often, with one of the Bravo sons. As if down an endless, dark tunnel, the words echoed in her head.

So. This was it. The moment she had so dreaded had

finally come. The truth had caught up with her. Mercy sat very still, waiting to feel…what? Guilt. Sadness. Something beyond this numb disbelief.

She was going to lose Luke now. She would have to give him up. For the sake of her family. To prove how much she loved them, to honor all that she owed them.

Mercy stared blankly at her mother. And as she stared, something changed within her. The change was shocking, enormous: a shift in her very view of the world.

Impossible. But yes, it was happening. It was real. She stared at her mother across the table and she felt the first wild, burning surge of rebellion.

I love him. The words were there. The *truth* was there, the basic fact that she had been avoiding, the central reality that up till now, she'd hardly dared give a name.

Love.

I love him and he's a fine man and why—why do I have to lose him?

The answer was pitifully simple.

Because she was a coward, someone willing to do whatever her family demanded, simply because they told her to. Someone willing to surrender her heart and her future happiness for the sake of an old bitterness that insanely refused to die.

No. It was wrong to let bitterness steal her love from her. Terribly wrong. And she was not going to let it happen.

Mercy sat straighter. "I love you, Mom. I love Dad and Elena. You've made my life a good one. You've given me love and support and the guiding hand I needed when I lost my first mother. I owe you so much. Everything. But I have to ask you, what are you saying? What do you want from me?"

Her mother blinked in surprise that Mercy would even have to ask such a question. "You know exactly what I want. I want you to honor your family. I want you to stop seeing Luke Bravo. I want you to stop now. Today."

"Why?" The word slipped out of her mouth and she could hardly believe she had asked it.

Luz gaped. "*¿Que?* You know why. He is our enemy."

"No. No, he's not. His grandfather was our enemy, yes. And his father, maybe, for firing you when you were working for him. But really, why was that so bad? After he fired you, you and dad worked out your problems. And since then, you've built a rich and prosperous life together. If you think about it, Luke's dad firing you was a good thing. It gave you another chance with Dad. And it made you get out there and make a go of it in business for yourself, on your own terms."

"You don't know what you're talking about."

"I don't? Then enlighten me, Mom. Make me understand."

"They killed your grandfather and your uncle Emilio, too."

"Please. You make their deaths sound like cold-blooded murder. And we both know they weren't. And Luke himself has never done harm to us. He's good. A good man."

"Your father would never—"

"Forget Dad for the moment."

"Forget *su papi?*" In horror, Luz whispered the words. "How can you say that?"

"What about you, Mom? How do you feel, really? Would it really be so hard for you to forget the past, to allow your daughter to find her happiness, to grab her love and hold him tight, to never let him go?"

Luz put her hands over her mouth. Above her beautiful French-manicured fingernails, her eyes were wide and full of fear. She sank back in her chair—and then crossed herself. *"Ah, madre dulce Maria."* She muttered more Spanish. Something about blame and punishment.

Mercy hated this, so much—to see her mother suffer this way. She had dreaded the coming of this day. But somehow, she hadn't expected Luz to plead with her like this, to be so frantic and fearful. Righteous anger, yes, and hard demands. But not this anguish, this obvious distress.

She knew she could stop her mother's suffering, knew how to make things okay again, if not all better. All she had to do was promise to give Luke up.

Give him up. It was what she had always known she would do if the family found out about their love affair.

But now that the moment was upon her, she couldn't make herself say the words, couldn't tell her mom she would end it with Luke. Now, to tell Luz she would say goodbye to Luke seemed terribly wrong. It seemed a capitulation to the deepest kind of lie—that a man could be defined as bad simply because of his last name.

"Mom." Mercy spoke gently. "Come on. *Escúcheme.* Listen to me. Please…"

Luz sighed and sadly shook her head. Then, at last, she smoothed her hair again and straightened her turquoise blouse. "All right. I'm listening. What?"

"Can you sit there and look me in the eye and tell me you really believe that Luke Bravo is our enemy because of things his grandfather did? I'm telling you, and I know it's true, that he's a good man."

Luz's gaze slid away. "It doesn't matter whether he's good or not. It matters that you are loyal to your family, to your people who love you and care for you and stand in support of you, no matter what."

"But I *am* loyal to my family. You know that I am."

Luz was shaking her head again. "Ah, *mija*…"

Mercy spoke gently. "If you could only set aside your senseless prejudice, Mom. If you could just see this situation clearly, for what it really is. I care for someone, someone who is a good person, someone who is more than just his last name."

"I do see it clearly—more clearly than you can ever know. And I see trouble. Big trouble coming. We need to stay away from them. We need to leave the Bravos alone."

"I don't think so. Not anymore—if we ever really did. Knowing Luke…it's changed me, Mom. I can't believe anymore that it has to be the way it's always been. I can see a better way, a new way. I think you could, too, if you would only let yourself."

Her mother refused to hear her. "No good can come from this. Please. For my sake and the sake of your family, consider what I ask of you. Consider your loyalties and your father's honor. Say goodbye to him. Tell him you don't want to see him again. It's not too late. You can just walk away. We can put this behind us. It can be as if you were never with him. Your father never has to know."

Somehow, Mercy got through the rest of the afternoon. She tried to put the confrontation with her mother out of her mind, to focus on the animals that needed her care.

She resisted the urge to call Luke and ask for comfort. Or even to call Elena for support. She didn't want to drag her sister into it again. And Luke, well, she would see him that evening. It would be better to wait until she was with him, until they could deal with it together, face-to-face.

The hours crawled by. At five-thirty, she finished treating a sick goat and drove home to clean up again. She called Luke as she was leaving her house.

"Mercy." The sound of his voice made her heart feel lighter.

"I'm a little late, I know. But I'll be there. I'm just getting in the pickup."

"I'm here. Waiting."

"And I'm so glad you are."

When she got to the ranch, she pulled up in the wide circular driveway in front of the big, white house. He was there, on the front veranda, in jeans and a worn chambray shirt with the sleeves rolled to his elbows, waiting for her. She grabbed her overnighter from the backseat, hooked her purse over her shoulder and jumped out.

She was up those wide steps so fast, her feet hardly touched the ground.

At the top, he caught her in his strong arms. He held on so tight, as if he knew what had happened that day without even being told, as if he knew that she needed his arms around her.

He pressed his warm lips to her temple. "I had this crazy fear that you wouldn't come tonight, that I would never see you again...."

She held him around the waist, her hands clasped at the small of his back, and she tipped her head up to look at him. "I'm here. Right here. And there are things, important things, that we need to talk about."

He touched her cheek. "Yeah. There are…" He took her arm and led her inside and up the central staircase to his suite of rooms, Lollie trailing behind.

Once they were in his sitting room with the door shut and the dog stretched out on the rug by the sofa, Mercy shook her head. "Oh, Luke. I don't know where to start."

He took her shoulders and stared hard into her eyes. "I'll start."

She gazed up at him, dread making a knot in her stomach. "What?"

"My father and I had a little talk last night."

"Oh, no…"

"Yeah." He told her what his father had said the night before. When he had finished, she told him about her lunch with her mom. Once she'd told it all, he released her shoulders and let his arms drop to his sides. He went to the wet bar in the corner, glancing back to ask, "Want something?"

"No. Thank you."

He dropped ice cubes into a tall glass and poured water over them. She waited, standing where he'd left her by the door, as he drank the water down. He set the empty glass on the bar's black marble counter.

And at last, he faced her directly again. "You think the 'friend' your mother mentioned is my dad?"

She shrugged. "I guess it's possible. Even probable. They may be enemies, but enemies have been known to unite for a common cause."

"A common cause," he repeated. "Like making sure that the two of us stop seeing each other immediately."

"Yeah. I can see them suspending hostilities long enough to make that happen."

He folded his arms across his chest and leaned against the bar. "So, then. I told my father to go to hell. What did you tell your mother?"

"Oh, Luke. Please. Don't look at me like that." She dared a step toward him.

He put up a hand and reminded her ruefully, "Waiting for an answer here…"

She stopped where she was and lifted her chin. "I always thought that when my parents found out and demanded I end it with us, I would. But today, when my mom begged me to break it off with you…" She let her voice trail off as she sought the right words to explain it to him.

His body tensed. "Mercy. Come on. Can't you see you're killing me? Put me out of my misery. It's the least you can do."

"Yes. All right. I told her no. I told her I wanted to be with you. That you're a good man and it's time we all got past this stupid feud."

His mouth was hanging open. "Would you say that again?"

"Oh, Luke…"

"You're serious. You told your mom you were sticking with me?"

She gave a low, trembling laugh. "Is that so surprising?"

"Well. Yeah. It is. It's a damn big shock, if you want to know the truth. I always thought, when you had to choose, it wouldn't go in my—in *our*—favor."

"Oh." She felt absurdly hopeful. And proud, too. "Well, I can see why you would have thought that. I mean, *I* thought the same thing. But as it turns out, we were both wrong."

A slow smile of relief and triumph curled his wonderful mouth. "Come here."

She didn't need to be told twice. She ran to him and he opened his strong arms to her.

The kiss they shared stole her breath and made her see stars. Then he scooped her up and carried her into the bedroom. He took off his boots and she kicked away her flats. And they lay down on the bed together.

He turned on his side and she tucked herself up against him, spoon fashion, taking his arm and wrapping it around her. She stroked the golden hairs on his corded forearm, thinking, *I love you,* but not quite able to say it.

Not *ready* to say it.

Not yet.

"I'm thinking another family dinner," he whispered against her hair. "We'll ask both families to come."

She took his hand and brought it to her breast. He opened his fingers and cupped her, so tenderly, through her clothes. "Maybe we should take it one family at a time. Get them used to the idea in stages."

He nuzzled her hair. "Good thinking. We don't want them killing each other."

"So maybe, as a start, you talk to your family. And I'll talk to mine. Separately, I mean. We'll make it clear to them that what we have together isn't going to just go away, that they have no right—let alone any real reason—to try and keep us apart. Once we've both made that step, we'll talk it over. We'll decide where to take it from there."

He pulled her closer against him. "You swear you won't crap out on me?"

She turned her head. His lips were waiting. "I do. I swear." She breathed the vow against his mouth. "No matter what happens, I will stick by you. I won't back down."

Chapter Ten

Mercy left the next morning at nine. For Luke, it was easier than it had ever been to let her go. As of the night before, he and Mercy were together. *Really* together. From now on, he wouldn't have to wonder if something would happen in the hours they were apart to make her decide to call it quits between them.

Caleb arrived just as he was walking her down the front steps. The Audi burned rubber, squealing to a stop next to Mercy's pickup. Luke shook his head at the sight. Caleb drove like there was no tomorrow.

His brother jumped out of the low black car and aimed his famous killer smile at Mercy. "Hey. Mercedes. Great to see you. How you been?"

Luke had his arm around her as they descended the wide front steps. He held her tighter when he felt her shy away. She sent him a chiding glance—and then a soft laugh escaped her. She swayed even closer to him.

"Hi, Caleb." She was still looking at him when she spoke to his brother. The intimate gleam in her eyes made his heart feel too big for his chest. "I'm doing fine. Really good."

Caleb asked, "Elena?"

"She's started her first year of teaching history to teenagers."

Caleb reached them midway between the steps and the vehicles. "Teaching teenagers. Sounds like living hell to me."

"She says she loves it."

"I'll bet she's good at it."

Luke cut through the chitchat. "So what's up, little brother?"

A lazy shrug. Maybe too lazy. "Just thought I'd drop by. See how you're doing…"

"Zita's got the coffee made. I'll be right in."

Caleb nodded at Mercy, ran up the front steps and into the house.

She turned into his arms. "You think maybe he's figured out that I spent the night?"

"It's a definite possibility." He took a lock of her midnight hair and brought it to his lips. Silky. Like the rest of her. "At least he's on our side."

She guided the strands free of his grip, smoothing them over her shoulder. "And Elena will be, too. We'll have support, at least."

"And each other."

"Each other, most of all." She kissed him goodbye—a deep, passionate kiss, with nothing held back. He stayed to watch her drive away, feeling certain that they were going to make it now, that nothing could stand in their way.

In the kitchen at the back of the house, Lollie was asleep in the corner and Caleb was drinking his coffee and munching a bagel with cream cheese. At the sight of Luke, he set down his bagel, saluted with his coffee cup—and started singing a pop song about young love.

Lollie lifted her head long enough to yawn, and Luke hid his grin. "You never could carry a tune." He went over to the counter and poured himself a cup.

Caleb said, "Dad threatened to punch my lights out yesterday."

Luke turned to face his brother. He sipped the dark brew. "I don't know if I should ask why."

"You should," Caleb answered cheerfully. "He was acting like a first-class ass all day. Barking at people in the sales meeting, growling at poor Mindy." Mindy was Davis's assistant.

"Mindy's used to him."

"Uh-uh. This was way worse than his usual I-rule-the-world-and-don't-you-forget-it routine. You would have had to be there to believe it. Finally, around three, I got him alone. I asked him what the hell his problem was."

Luke took a chair at the table. "Let me guess. He told you that Mercy and I were seeing each other."

Caleb nodded. "He tells me about Mercy like it's the worst thing that could ever happen. Armageddon. The end of days. Then he waits for me to say how terrible it is, to promise that I'll go and talk some sense into you—and if you don't listen, beat the crap out of you."

Luke let out a dry chuckle. "As if you could take me."

Caleb's green eyes gleamed. "You know I could. But why would I want to? I think it's terrific about you and Mercy and I told Dad so. It's terrific and about damn time somebody stood up and said, enough! Things have got to change."

Luke grunted and sipped more coffee. "I'm thinking when you get tired of sales, politics is your game. You'll be great on the stump."

"Go ahead, mock me. I'm on your side, big brother. That's all I'm saying." Caleb bit off a hunk of bagel and chewed with gusto.

"Thanks," Luke said mildly. "I have a feeling we'll need all the support we can get. Mercy's mom found out. She begged Mercy to dump me and do it now. Luz called on the holy Virgin and predicted big trouble if Mercy stuck with me."

Caleb swallowed the wad of bagel and cream cheese. Hard. "That does it. I'm asking Elena out."

"Caleb—"

"Uh-uh. Don't try to talk me out of it. She's a great girl. And why shouldn't I take her to a damn movie if she's willing to go?"

"I'm only saying that it's not like you're wild for her or anything. Why go there? If you really wanted to ask her out so much, you would have done it by now—no matter what I said to try and stop you."

"It's the principle of the thing. If I want to ask her out and she says yes, we have a right to spend an evening together. It's ridiculous to say we don't. And I will go public, upfront. Does she live on her own now?"

"Why?"

"Just answer the question."

"No. She's still at home—I think Mercy said she'd be there until her condo's finished next month."

"Perfect. I'll march up to her door and I'll ask her out, with Javier and Luz standing right there."

"Caleb. Man, ease it down a notch." It was kind of scary, really. Luke had never seen his smooth-talking brother so impassioned about anything.

"I'm doing it," said Caleb. "I'm doing it today, this morning, as soon as I finish this bagel. So stop trying to talk me out of it."

"I'm only asking you why you want to go stirring up trouble for yourself and for Elena when you don't even care that much?"

"You don't get it, big brother. I do care. I care about *you.* I see you look at Mercy and I watch the way she looks at you and I think, damn, *that's it!* That's what life's all about. That's what makes it all worthwhile. I'm willing to stand up for that, for the two of you, for what you've got together."

"You don't have to confront Javier Cabrera to stand up for us."

"I'm not confronting him. I'm asking his daughter out—and I'm doing it respectfully, too, right out in the open. Maybe he'll be more rational than his wife and our father. Maybe he'll invite me in and tell me he's ready to be a bigger man than Davis Bravo."

"I don't like it."

"Don't worry. I'll be a gentleman. I've got a good feeling about this, Luke. I really do."

"Do me one favor."

Caleb's eyes narrowed to warning slits. "Don't try and stop me, Luke. My mind's made up."

"Just call me when you leave their house, will you? Let me know if Javier Cabrera chased you off his property with a shotgun so I can pass the news on to Mercy."

"There's not going to be any shotgun. Don't worry."

"Just call me, okay?"

"Absolutely. You can count on me."

Caleb left half an hour later, undeterred by any of Luke's arguments against his wild-ass plan to date Elena Cabrera for the sake of true love and freedom from family tyranny. He was heading straight for Luz and Javier's, the address of which he'd easily found by looking them up on his iPhone.

As soon as he was out the door, Luke called Mercy to give her a heads-up as to what was about to happen at her parents' house. He got voice mail when he tried her cell, so he left a message and called her house, where he got her answering machine.

She was on call for the weekend, so she'd probably gone out to some ranch somewhere to doctor up somebody's livestock. He left a message on the house phone, too. And then he went out to the stables to run a couple of spirited yearlings through their paces, his cell in a belt holster, so he would know if she called.

Mercy didn't call. But a little before eleven, Caleb did.

Luke was in the tack room at the time, hanging up his equipment. "Well?"

"Do I have the instinct for people or what?" Caleb sounded lighthearted. And smug.

"Speak. Tell me."

"Piece of cake. Luz acted squirrelly, kind of freaked out and strange. But Elena seemed happy enough to see me."

"And Javier?"

"Like I expected, he's a bigger man than Dad."

"You're serious? He was okay with you and Elena going out?"

"He was very…solemn. Luke, I really like him. He shook my hand and said he was glad I'd come. That in the last few years, he'd begun to think about things differently. He said that he thought that peace between our families would be a fine thing—his words. A fine thing."

Luke had never expected that Javier Cabrera might end up an ally in this. Light-headed with surprise and relief, he dropped to a hay bale. "So then. I guess you're going out with Elena?"

"Yes, I am. Tonight, as a matter of fact. Dinner and a show."

Mercy didn't check her cell messages until noon. She got one from Luke asking her to call as soon as she could.

Something in his tone had her feeling nervous. She called him right back and he picked up on the second ring.

"Hey," he said, his deep voice sending the usual warm shiver through her. "You working?"

"Just finished at a pig farm up by San Marcos. A muddy job if there ever was one. On my way back to SA now. I had my phone on vibrate—in my bag. So I didn't know you'd called. Anything important? You sounded kind of worried in that message you left."

He laughed. "I guess I was. But not anymore. I'm shocked as hell. But not the least worried."

"Luke. Don't tease. Tell me. What's going on?"

"Well, Caleb had it out with Dad over you and me. He was so mad at our father, he decided to ask your sister out."

Mercy's mouth went dry. "Hold on." Suddenly, her hands were shaking. She shouldn't be driving and she knew it. She steered the car to the side of the road and stopped.

Luke demanded, "Mercy? You there?"

"Yes. Right here." She swallowed—and told herself she would not overreact. "Can you talk to Caleb? Tell him it would be better if he stayed out of it?"

"Mercy. Listen. It worked out fine."

Cars whizzed past. Mercy stared blindly out the windshield at the rolling Texas hills. "He already asked her?"

"Yeah. He went to your parents' house—"

"Sweet Maria…"

"—and it was fine."

She tore off the band that held her hair and then raked her fingers back through the heavy, mud-spattered mass. "No. Not really. Fine?"

"Fine. Yeah. Really. Your father shook his hand and said it was time for there to be peace between our families."

Shocked and a little dizzy with it, Mercy rested her forehead on the steering wheel. "Oh, Luke. I can hardly believe it. That's wonderful."

"Yeah. Just what I thought. A big step in the right direction."

She sat up straighter. "Did Elena say yes?"

"They're going out tonight."

"And my mom? Did she change her attitude, once she learned my dad was fine with it?"

"I don't think so. Caleb said she seemed freaked out."

Mercy didn't get it. "But if my dad's all right with it…"

"I know. It makes no sense. But if you think about it,

there's nothing sensible about people hating other people just because of their last name."

"I need to clean up. And then I'll go over there."

"Call me."

"I will."

They said goodbye. Before she pulled back out into traffic, Mercy tried Elena's cell. No answer.

She left a message in voice mail. "It's Mercy. Give me a call."

And then she tried the number at the house. After four rings, the machine picked up. Mercy disconnected that call without saying anything. Strange they didn't answer. She was definitely going over there as soon as she'd washed up.

At her house, she grabbed a quick shower and an apple, which she ate for lunch on the way over to her parents' place. When she got there, she saw her father's Cadillac in the three-car driveway. She parked beside it. Trying to tamp down her anxiety, to tell herself that there was nothing to worry about, that everything was working out much better than she'd ever dared to dream it might, she hurried across the driveway and along the meandering front walk to the wide stone porch and the arched, beautifully carved front door.

The heavy door was open a crack, which she found odd. She grasped the iron latch and pushed it inward. That was when she heard the shouting.

"Puta!" It was her father's voice. A stream of crude Spanish followed.

Her mother cried, "Javier, no…"

Mercy was inside by then. *"Mami…"* She stepped out of the entry hall and saw them in the living room.

Tears streamed down her mother's face. Mercy stared in horror, rooted to the spot, her stunned brain trying to process what was happening before her.

Between sobs that shook her slender frame, Luz pleaded with her husband. "Javier, I beg you. Don't hate me. Try to understand…"

"Understand?" Javier laughed. It was an ugly, furious sound. "*Comprendo todo.* I understand everything now, too well." And he spat at her. He spat full in her face.

She cried out again, a low, trembling, wounded cry. But she didn't move. She only stood there, staring at him through streaming eyes, making no attempt to wipe it away. And then he raised his hand and he struck her, full across the face.

With a wild cry, she fell.

The sight spurred Mercy to action, at last. "*Papi!*" she shouted. "*Papi*, stop."

Javier whirled on her, his eyes feral and blazing as those of a mad bull. Never in her life had she seen her kind, gentle father behave this way. He shook his head as if to clear it. And then, letting out another stream of bad words in Spanish, he barreled toward her.

With a cry, Mercy stepped to the side. He kept on going, stalking past her and out the door, not once looking back. She heard him get in his car and start up the engine. Rubber squealed as he backed and drove away.

Luz lay curled in a ball on the floor, sobbing.

Mercy went to her. "Oh, *Mami*…" She knelt beside her and gathered her into her arms, cradling her, rocking her, stroking her back and kissing her hair. "Shh, shh. It's okay, okay…" She said the words and knew they were hollow. At that moment, she couldn't help wondering if things would ever be okay again.

Eventually, Luz allowed Mercy to help her up and lead her to the sofa. Her lip was cut and swelling, dripping blood. Mercy went to the half bath near the entry hall and ran cool water on a washcloth. She took it back to Luz.

"Here, *Mami*." Her mother stared up at her blankly, blood dripping onto her pretty silk blouse as another sob trembled through her. Mercy pointed to her mouth. "For your lip…"

Luz took the cloth and pressed it to the injury. She was still crying—soft, hopeless sobs. Mercy sat beside her and rubbed her back some more, until she quieted a little.

Finally, Mercy dared to ask, "Elena?"

"Upstairs," her mother whispered around the washcloth.

"Is she okay?"

"No. *Sí.* I think so…"

Mercy took that to mean her sister was at least physically all right. She decided to stick with Luz for now, before she went up to check on Elena. Luz seemed so pitiful, the look in her eyes spoke of hopeless desolation. It didn't feel right to leave her alone until she had calmed at least a little.

Another fit of crying took Luz. She moaned and sagged toward Mercy. Mercy gathered her in, held her, whispered numb reassurances until the crying eased again.

Finally, Luz began to talk. "Ah, *mija*." She let go of Mercy and sagged back against the cushions. Mercy offered her a tissue from the box on the coffee table. Luz waved it away with the bloody washcloth. "I knew this would happen," she cried. "When I learned you were seeing that Bravo man, I knew my sins were going to catch up with me. The guilt…ah, *mija,* you'll never know. Guilt like knives, slicing deep in my poor heart. I thought I had conquered it—my shame—that I had left it behind long ago. But shame is never really gone. Only buried. Waiting for someone to dig it from the grave again. Since Friday, when I saw your love for Davis Bravo's son shining in your eyes, when I knew you cared too much to give him up…I couldn't sleep. I prayed. I asked forgiveness. I almost started to think it would be…bearable. That I could do it. Put on my bravest face, give you my blessing to go with your love, and go on living this beautiful, happy lie with my husband, who I do love, *mija.* I love him so much. I always have. I thought it would work out. I thought it would be okay. But then, today…" Her voice faded to nothing. She stared into the middle distance and a hard shiver took her.

Mercy waited. The waiting was terrible. She knew the awful truth already. What she'd witnessed between her mother and father had done it, snapped all the random pieces of the puzzle into place. Still, she needed to hear the words from her mother's bloody, swollen mouth. She needed to be certain before she went upstairs to try and comfort her poor baby sister.

Finally, she prompted, "You're talking about Caleb? Is that what you mean? That he was here? That he asked Elena to go out with him and she said yes?"

A keening cry escaped Luz. She tossed the wet cloth away, wrapped her arms around herself and rocked back and forth on the sofa cushions, staring blankly straight ahead, her nose and eyes streaming, the tears mingling with the blood still dribbling over her chin from her cut lip.

"Yes," she cried. "Oh, yes. Caleb Bravo knocking on our door today was my worst nightmare come to find me and make me pay for my mortal sin. But I thought it might still be all right. That Javier would surely forbid Elena to go out with a Bravo, that maybe Elena might listen to him. But no. Everything went wrong. Your father spoke gently. He said it was all right with him, that he was ready to let the old hatred go. And Elena told Caleb Bravo yes, she would go out with him. Tonight. Don't you see, Mercy? I couldn't allow that. By all that is sacred, such a wrong cannot be." Luz groped wildly for Mercy's hand.

Mercy gave it. She made herself speak calmly. "I'm here, Mom. Right here. Go ahead. Please. Tell me the rest."

Luz squeezed her fingers and swallowed a sob. "Caleb left. And Elena went up to her room. And Javier kissed me, such a tender kiss, and said he had a few hours' work he needed to do. The moment he was gone, I went up to Elena. I tried to talk reasonably to her, to tell her it really wasn't a good idea for her to go out with Caleb, that in spite of what her dad had said, it would only make trouble if she went out with a Bravo. I asked her to call him and tell him she had changed her mind. But you know how she is. So stubborn. She refused. And then I was begging her. And then I was yelling at her. And then, before I knew it, the words were there, in my mouth, demanding to be said. I let them out. I told her…"

"That Davis Bravo is her real father?" Mercy's heart

felt like a stone in her chest. She pulled her hand free of her mother's grip.

Luz shuddered. And then she moaned. And then, at last, she confessed it. "Yes. It's true. Caleb is her half brother. Elena is Davis Bravo's child."

Chapter Eleven

Though Mercy had known it already, to hear it from her mother's lips was a terrible thing.

"H-how…?" she heard herself stammer. "Why?"

By then, her mother's eyes were dry. But the pain in them was hard to look at. She answered Mercy in a low, flat voice, telling her how it had been all those years ago, when Javier couldn't find work and they needed money so badly.

"I was so angry—more angry than Javier—at those Bravos for stealing so much. For taking our home and our heritage, all that should have been ours. And Javier was doubly angry. Because he had given me no babies, though we both wanted little ones so much. There was…tension between us. Trouble, you know? And one day, I was so angry, I went to the Bravo company building downtown and I asked to speak with the boss. Davis came to talk to me, instead of his father, who was still running the company then. I told him he should be ashamed. That his people had taken everything from us…"

"And he gave you a job?"

She nodded and swallowed, hard, on a sob. "He asked me if I could type and I told him of course. He said, 'Then come to work for me. We'll put this feud behind us.' I…took his offer. I knew I shouldn't have. But we did need the money. I thought that maybe…I don't know. I don't remember why I took the job. It was a challenge Davis made me, a challenge I accepted." She hung her head. "Javier ordered me to quit. I refused. We had a terrible fight and he left me. Months went by. It was…strictly professional between me and Davis. But I was lonely and angry at Javier. And Davis—he loved his wife, but she was busy with all the babies he had given her. He was lonely, too. Sometimes, he would call me into his office and we would talk. Just talk. And then, one day, he reached for me. I went to him. It lasted for three weeks. And we both knew how wrong it was, hated ourselves for betraying the ones we loved. We ended it. We tried afterward to pretend it hadn't happened, to go on as before. But that was no good."

"You quit and agreed to say he had fired you."

"Yes. That way I could get unemployment at least. Not long after I quit working for Davis, Javier came back to me. And then I found there was a baby coming. I knew it was too soon to be Javier's. And I was a coward. I wanted happiness, a life with the man I loved. I lied. The oldest lie. I told him Elena was born early. He believed me. He wanted a child as much as I did. Our years of happiness began…."

"Does Davis Bravo know that Elena is his?"

Luz pressed her lips together and shook her head hard. "I told no one. I planned to take the secret to my grave." She touched a finger to her swollen lip. "But I was frantic. What if Elena and Caleb…" She closed her eyes. "No."

"And…Davis is the one who called you, who said that Luke and I had been seen together?"

"*Sí.* He thought that I should know. He said that your being with Luke would only cause trouble in so many ways, that it was better to leave the past behind. And how could we do that if our children bound their lives together?"

Luke. Saying his name—hearing it on her mother's lips. It hurt. So much. What would happen to their love now?

Mercy pushed the question from her mind. It wasn't the time to face it. Later. Not now, with her family shattering before her eyes.

Luz continued in a small, torn voice, "And then Caleb came asking for Elena. I couldn't bear the thought of what might happen between the two of them. So I said the truth, I told Elena."

"And Dad overheard."

Luz nodded. "He'd come back. I don't know why. Maybe he forgot something. He must have heard me yelling and come upstairs to see what the shouting was about. I told Elena my secret. And then I turned around and Javier was standing there in the doorway—Ah, *Dios mio.*" She put her head in her hands. "I will die with that look he wore burned in my brain. I have lost him, lost my love. He will never, ever return to me…."

Mercy stared at her mother's bent head, out of comfort to give her, out of lying, gentle words to say. Luz was right. Her betrayal was too enormous, too far-reaching. She couldn't imagine how Javier would ever be able forgive such treachery from the woman he had loved and trusted above all for almost thirty years.

"And why would he come back to you?" The voice came from the wide arch that led to the dining room. It was Elena, dry-eyed, her face a careful mask, strictly composed. She had two suitcases, one in either hand. "You don't deserve forgiveness. There aren't any words bad enough for what you've done."

Luz gasped. She cried, "Elena, *por favor.*" And she started to stand, arms reaching. "I never meant to—"

"Stop. Save your lies. You did what you did. And while you were at it, you stole from me. You took the only father I've ever known. I saw his face, too. I saw the way he couldn't look at me." Elena waved a dismissing hand. "Don't even try to come close to me. You don't know what I might do."

Mercy warned softly, "Elena, don't…"

Her sister shifted those too-calm eyes her way. A slow, controlled sigh escaped her. "You're right. We don't need to get into it. She knows what she did." Elena hefted her suitcases. "I'll be staying with you until my place is finished."

"Of course."

Luz collapsed in a fresh fit of weeping.

Mercy took her in her arms. She spoke to her sister over their mother's shaking shoulders. "You've got your key?" At Elena's nod, she suggested, "Go ahead, then. I'll stay here for a while."

Elena's eyes filled with sudden tears. Furiously, she blinked them back and, with a curt nod, she left. Mercy held on to Luz, rocking her, making tender noises as Luz cried out her shame and her loss.

Finally, Luz ran dry of tears, she lifted her head. "Ah, *mija*…"

Mercy kept an arm around her. The two sat side-by-side, their heads tipped close in a bleak silence. A sad calm after a terrible storm.

In time, Luz pulled free of Mercy's arms. She glanced down at her ruined, bloodstained blouse. "I think I need to clean up a little." She rose.

"Can I help?"

She bent to brush a tender hand across Mercy's cheek. "No, *gracias*. I can rinse my own face." She went to the guest bath.

Mercy waited anxiously for her to come out. She was just about to go tap on the bathroom door, to make certain Luz was all right, when she emerged.

She came and sat back down beside Mercy. "I'm better now," she said. "I'm just fine." They both knew she wasn't.

Yes, she'd rinsed the tears and the blood from her face and tried to clean the bloodstains from her blouse. But the stains were still there. The tender flesh beneath her eyes was puffy and blue-shadowed. Mercy thought she looked worn, haggard. As if she had aged a decade since the day before, when they'd met in Market Square for lunch.

"Go, Mercedes." Luz tipped her head toward the door. "Go to your sister. She needs you now. She tries to be brave. But we both saw her pain."

Mercy felt the tears rising in the back of her throat. "Oh, *Mami,* I don't know if I should leave you."

"Go."

"I don't want to leave you alone."

Luz smiled the saddest, loneliest smile. "But I *am* alone, *mija*. I will need to learn to get used to it."

"You wouldn't…" Mercy didn't know how to say it. It seemed wrong even to hint at it.

Luz laughed, low. A sound of infinite sadness. "No, *mija*. Your sister has called my sins beyond forgiving and that may be so. But I will bear them. To try to escape them in the way you're thinking, to do so much more damage to my family than I've *already* done…no. It's time for me to face my sins, to do penance for them. And with the help of God and the holy Virgin, I will. I swear to you. I will. The truth is out. Never again will I seek a way to hide from it or to make it go away."

At home, Mercy found her sister crying. Elena sat on the rug in the living room, legs crossed, cradling Orlando between her knees, mourning her loss.

Mercy got a box of Kleenex and sat with her. When Elena wound down a little, Mercy offered the box.

"I hate her," Elena muttered, and blew her nose. Orlando lay half in her lap. He let out a whine of doggy understanding. Elena gave him an absentminded rub behind the ear. She slanted a glance at Mercy. "Do you think you should have left her?"

Needing the contact, Mercy reached out and smoothed a hand down her sister's beautiful hair. "She wanted me to come to you. To comfort you."

"But I don't think she ought to be alone now. What if she—?"

"No. She won't."

"How can you be sure?"

"Because she told me she wouldn't. And I believed her."

Elena still looked doubtful. "If you think so…"

"I do. Please. Don't worry she'll do harm to herself. She won't, okay?"

Elena's shoulders slumped. She hung her head and her hair fell forward, making a curtain around the sad-eyed Orlando. He stretched his neck to lick her face. "Oh, Orlando…" She caught his muzzle between her hands, pressed her cheek to his. He whined in sympathy again.

Mercy sought the right words and found none. "I wish I knew what to say. I wish I had a way to make it all better."

Elena straightened her shoulders. "Nothing can make it better—except maybe time. But if I didn't have you to turn to now, Mercy mine, I don't know. That would make it all so much worse."

"I'm here. *Siempre.*"

"Good." Elena rubbed her eyes and blew out a hard breath. "All this. The destruction of our family…for what? It was only a date, you know? I wasn't in love with him or anything. Since she went on with that giant lie for so long, why couldn't she just leave it, just wait and see that it was no big deal?"

"Guilt." Mercy said the word softly. "She was frantic. She found out about me and Luke yesterday. We had lunch. She begged me to end it with him."

Elena made a low sound and for the first time in what seemed like forever, her full lips curved in a near-smile. "So. You and Luke *are* back together, then. I kind of thought so."

But could they stay together, after this? Mercy didn't want to think about it. Not now. "Are you still going out with Caleb?"

Elena gasped. "No."

"Will you tell him why?"

"I hardly know him. Can you see me telling him I can't go out with him because his father slept with my mother and it turns out I'm his long-lost half sister?"

Mercy winced. "Guess not."

"I'll have to back out, that's all. Tell him I've changed my mind."

"Did he give you a phone number, in case you had to reach him before tonight?"

Elena dug in a back pocket and pulled out a card. She held it up. Mercy grabbed the phone from the coffee table and handed it over. Elena made the call. She nodded at Mercy when Caleb answered.

"Hi. It's Elena. Listen, Caleb. As it turns out, I can't go out with you tonight... No, I don't think so. I just don't think it would be such a great idea, you know?" She was silent again. Faintly, Mercy could hear Caleb's voice on the other end of the line. Elena cleared her throat. "Yes. All right. I will. Goodbye, then." She pushed the off button and heaved a huge sigh.

"Well?"

"He was...nice. He told me he didn't understand, but if I felt so strongly, well, what could he say?"

"So, then. That's settled."

Elena stared at her mournfully. "I can't stop thinking about *Papi.* I hope he's all right."

"We can try his cell..."

Elena passed the phone to Mercy. "You'd better do

it. I don't think he wants to talk to me. And I can't bear to talk to him. Not right now."

"Elena, it's not your fault. You did nothing wrong."

She petted Orlando with slow, loving strokes. "I know that. But I just think it's better if you make the call."

So Mercy called Javier's cell. The call went straight to voice mail. She left a brief message. "It's me, Mercy. Just wanted to…see how you're doing. Call me, please." She hung up. And she tried his office number. The answering service picked up and took her message.

The sisters looked at each other. At last, Elena said, "Please, will you go to his office and check? He wouldn't answer on the weekend, anyway. The calls go straight to the service. But he's probably there. Where else would he go?"

Away, Mercy thought. *Far, far away.* She said, "You're right. I'll check." She set the phone back on the coffee table and stood. "Will *you* be okay?"

Elena gazed up at her. Orlando, too. "I'll…survive," she said. "Right now, I'll get busy. I'll unpack."

"Good idea. The guestroom bed is all made."

"I saw. Go. Find him. Call me after you talk to him."

Mercy's cell vibrated while she was driving to Cabrera Construction. She picked it up from the tray between the seats to glance at the display.

Luke.

The sight of his name as the phone buzzed in her hand made her want to cry. But she supposed there had been more than enough crying for one day. She set the phone down and let the call go to voice mail. It wasn't right, to blow him off like that. But she hardly knew what she would say if she tried to talk to him right then.

In the space of a couple of hours, her whole world had changed. The family that had sheltered her, loved her, cherished her—it was blown apart, damaged, she feared, beyond repair. Luz. Javier. Her beloved Elena. Their lives would never be the same. And Luke's father was complicit—instrumental, even—in the destruction.

Luke. Just thinking his name caused an ache in her heart. She didn't know how much she could tell him. It didn't seem her place, somehow, to reveal to him the unbelievable truth. For her family's sake. *And* his. She didn't even know his mother. But she doubted Aleta Bravo would be any happier over this revelation than Javier had been. It could shatter Luke's family, too—or at least, destroy his parents' long, successful marriage.

Mercy was a loyal daughter to the core. But revenge had never been her way. She found she ached for the Bravos and what this might do to them, almost as much as she hurt for her own people.

Maybe that was because she loved Luke now. It was impossible to hate his people, loving him as she did. She didn't want them to suffer as her family suffered—not even Davis Bravo, whom she would really like to call a whole bunch of ugly names and then punch square in the jaw.

No. She didn't know if she could stand to be the bearer of the terrible news. And she would have to consult with Elena first, anyway. Her sister was the innocent victim in this. Elena deserved to be consulted about whom to tell and how much. Maybe—even likely—someday she would want to confront the man who had given her life. But Mercy didn't think that was going to happen soon.

The offices of Cabrera Construction were in a former used car lot, a half a block's worth of parking, with a large, flat-roofed building in the center, which once had been the lot's showroom and sales offices. Mercy pulled to a stop in front of the building and got out of her pickup. The place looked deserted. The front was all windows. No movement inside.

A walk around the building proved her father couldn't be there. His Cadillac wasn't in the lot. There was just one car, a blue late-model SUV. She recognized it as belonging to her dad's secretary, Marcella, who often came in on Saturdays. Marcella liked to catch up on her paperwork when the place was nice and quiet. Just in case the secretary might have heard from him, Mercy went ahead and tried the steel door at the back of the building. Locked. So she pressed the buzzer to the left of the door.

Marcella came. She pushed the door wide. "Mercy. Hi."

"My father…has he been here?"

The older woman nodded. It seemed to Mercy that there was concern in her eyes. "He was here."

To confirm what she already knew, she asked, "But he's gone now?"

"Yes. He gave me a letter for you."

A letter. A knotted fist of dread clenched hard, in her belly. Why not just call her? Why not just pick up the phone when she had called him? "Could I have it then, please?"

"Of course. Come in. I'll get it."

Mercy followed Marcella inside. She waited in the short hallway just inside the door, reluctant, for no logical reason, to go farther. In less than a minute, Marcella returned with an envelope. Mercy took it in numb fingers. "How long ago was he here?"

Marcella frowned. She glanced at her watch. "He left less than an hour ago."

"Did he…say anything?"

"He said he would be taking a few days off. And that I could call his cell if there were any problems. He seemed…well, upset about something. Shaken, you know?" When Mercy nodded, she added, "He went to his office after he told me about his taking time off. In ten minutes or so, he came out and gave me the letter. He said when you came here, I should give it to you." Mercy wondered how he could have known that she would be the one to come looking for him. Marcella said, "Then he left. Mercy, has something bad happened?"

"It's…a family problem. Please don't worry. We're all well. It's only something we need to work out, that's all."

"Please don't hesitate to call if there's anything I can do."

Mercy thanked her and went back around the building to her pickup. She got in and shut the door.

And then she stared at the envelope. Plain. White. With her name scrawled on the front in her father's bold hand.

She considered waiting to open it until she got home to Elena. But no. He had written it to *her.* She ought to read it first. There might even be something inside that she wouldn't want Elena to see. She couldn't imagine their father being cruel to poor Elena, who was in no way at fault here. But when a man's trust and love were shattered, well, it was hard to guess the things that he might do.

So, with shaking hands, she tore open the envelope and read it right there in the pickup.

Mercedes,
It's easier for me to write this to you. I wouldn't
know what to say to your mother or to Elena. Not
now. The wound is too fresh. And I am guessing,
anyway, that Elena or your mother will be sending
you here to look for me.
   I must tell you that I love you and your sister
and I will always be your papi. But right now, I
will be needing a little time alone. I hope you
understand. Tell them I am safe and well. Please
don't worry for me.
   Take care of your mother.
Love,
Dad.

"But where would he go?" Elena demanded when
Mercy got back home and showed her the letter.

"I don't know." They were in the spare room—
Elena's room now. Mercy sank to the edge of the bed.
"A motel near his office. The other side of the world.
Anywhere, I suppose."

"This scares me."

"He wrote that he was safe and well."

"I don't care what he wrote. I hate it."

"Oh, Elena. I hate it, too. But he says he'll be all
right. We just have to trust that." Her phone started vi-
brating. She took it out and checked the display. Luke.
Again. Her heart ached. She set it on the dresser. In a
moment, the low buzz went silent.

"Who was that?"

"It doesn't matter," she baldly lied.

Elena dropped down next to her. "Who?"

Mercy sighed. "Luke. It was Luke. I don't know… how to talk to him, what to say to him."

Elena leaned her head on Mercy's shoulder. "Do you love him?" She asked the question so softly, on a breath.

"Yes. With all my heart."

"Then don't be cruel. Call him."

"You didn't hear me."

"Yes, I did."

"And tell him what, then?"

"I don't know. The truth, maybe."

Mercy pulled away and waited for Elena to meet her eyes. "You mean that? Are you ready for him to know he has another sister—you? Are you ready to deal with whatever happens once he knows?"

Elena gave a low, tired-sounding chuckle. "Well, I have to admit. I'd like a day or two to think it over, to let the dust settle a little before I decide what I want to do next."

"And that's why I'm not taking his calls. Because when I do talk to him, I'll either have to lie—or tell him what's happened. Neither option is attractive."

"You can't hide from him, though. It's only going to make him come looking for you."

Elena was right. Mercy still had the cell in her hand. She punched the call-back button.

Elena stood. "Shall I go?" she asked softly.

Mercy shook her head.

And then he was on the line. "Mercy." Her heart ached just to hear his voice. She wanted him with her. She wanted to hold him so tight, to close her eyes and have it be yesterday again, when all they had to worry about was how to reveal their love to their families. "Damn it to hell. Where are you?"

"At home."

"I called and called. Are you—?"

"I'm fine. Truly. I'm so sorry I didn't call. Something came up. A family problem."

"What problem?"

"It's…I don't want to go into it. I'm just…I'm sorry. I should have called."

"I heard from Caleb again. Your sister backed out on him. She said she'd changed her mind about going out with him, that she didn't think it was a good idea, after all."

"Yes, um, she told me that."

He swore low. "Mercy, what's going on? You didn't answer my calls. Now you sound really strange. You're freaking me out here."

"I said I'm sorry. I don't know what else to tell you."

He swore again. A really bad word. "Stay there. I'm on my way."

"No!"

A silence. Then, through gritted teeth, "What is going on?"

"Please." She met her sister's worried gaze. Uh-uh. She didn't want to deal with him at her house, where Elena had taken sanctuary. Elena didn't need that, not today, at least. "I'll come to you. At the ranch."

"When?"

"Right now. I'll leave right now."

"Mercy, I don't—"

"I'll be there. Just wait for me. I'm coming to you, I'll be there soon."

"I don't like this."

"Please stop worrying. I'm on my way."

She hung up before he could ask more questions. And she and Elena stared at each other helplessly.

Finally, in a small voice, her sister said, "I'm so sorry to put you in such a bad position."

"Hey." Mercy tried to speak lightly. "I guess it's just what happens when Bravos and Cabreras mix."

"No." Elena shook her head. Hard. "Don't even joke about it. We're better than that. *Beyond* that. Whatever happens, we won't ever go back to hating a person because of something their father or their grandfather did."

Love rose in Mercy then. Fierce and strong. "I'm so proud that you're my sister."

Elena gave a wry laugh. "Good. Because if you think about it, *I'm* what happens when Bravos and Cabreras mix." The laugh faded. A single tear slid down her cheek.

"Oh, Elena. Don't cry…."

Elena swiped the tear away and held out her hand. Mercy took it. Elena asked, "What will you tell him?"

"Nothing. I swear to you. Only what I already told him—that it's a family problem and I can't go into it."

Elena gazed at her pleadingly. "I shouldn't ask that of you, to lie to your love for me—but I am." She let go of Mercy's hand. "I only…I need some time, you know? To decide what to do next, to figure out where I go from here."

"I understand. And you have my word that I won't tell him."

"Thank you."

"Will you be all right alone?"

"If it gets too bad, I'll hold on to Orlando." The dog,

on the rug near her feet, looked up at the sound of his name and wagged his scraggly tail.

"I won't be long."

"Take your time. Stay all night if you want to. Go."

"Someone should check on *Mami*…"

"I'll give her a call. In a while, I promise. Now I mean it, go. The poor man. He's probably going crazy waiting for you to get there."

Chapter Twelve

Luke was practically crawling out of his own skin waiting for Mercy to show up. He paced the floor of the main sitting room at the front of the house, ears tuned for the sound of her pickup arriving.

When Zita stuck her head in to ask if he would be alone for dinner, he barked at her, "How the hell would I know—and why exactly should I care?"

Her dark eyes went wide and she fell all over herself apologizing. "Oh! So sorry. So sorry to disturb you…"

Way to go, Bravo, abusing poor Zita. He put up a hand and said gently, "No. *I'm* the one who's sorry. I've…got something on my mind, that's all. I shouldn't have jumped on you. Just make enough for two and leave it in the fridge, will you? And after that, you're free for the weekend." She had Sundays and Mondays off, as a rule.

Zita thanked him and left him alone.

The huge, high-ceilinged room felt too cramped to contain him. He flung back the doors to the foyer and strode to the front door. Lollie, who'd been stretched out near the marble fireplace, got up and followed him. He threw the front door wide open and went outside to wait. Lollie flopped down out of the way as he paced some more.

He was leaning against one of his grandfather's ridiculous white pillars when she finally drove up and stopped several yards from the front steps. She got out and came around the front of the vehicle toward him. He drank in the sight of her: all in one piece.

Worry had been eating him alive the whole afternoon. And now she was finally there, now he knew she was safe, his anxiety turned to relief—and the powerful need to have her in his arms.

She spotted him waiting in the shadow of the deep veranda. "Luke…" And she ran up the steps toward him. "I'm so sorry…"

He reached out and grabbed her and hauled her close to him. She gasped as she came up hard against him. "I don't want to hear that you're sorry."

"But I—"

"Shh. Don't talk. Not yet." He lowered his mouth and claimed her lips.

She stiffened—but then she sighed. Her body went easy in his arms. He kissed her deeply, tasting her. It soothed him, that kiss, eased his lingering apprehensions.

He had questions for her. Several. But they could wait until he had her inside. He lifted his head, but only long enough to mutter, "I missed you. So damn much." And then, before she could reply, he kissed her again.

The next time he lifted his head, he grabbed her hand. "Come on."

She said nothing, which was fine with him. The dog trailing behind them, he led her in the door and up the stairs and down the hall to his bedroom suite. Lollie went to her favorite spot by the sofa, walked in a circle, and dropped down with a snort.

Luke took Mercy's face between his hands. "You scared me."

"I'm s—"

He put a finger against her mouth. "Uh-uh. Don't say it. No more damn apologies." He had her backed against the door. He braced his hands to either side of her flushed, beautiful face. "What's happened with your family?"

"Oh, Luke. I…"

"What? Tell me."

"I'm sor…" She caught herself in mid-apology. "I can't. I can't talk about it. Not right now. I do wish I could." Those black eyes pleaded for him to understand.

Understand what? She hadn't told him anything. And the relief he'd felt at the sight of her outside was becoming something else. Fear. Was he losing her, then, after all? Was this it, the end between them—now, today?

He demanded, "Why did Elena back out on Caleb?"

She made a whimpering sound. "Luke. Please. Don't."

He forced himself to ask the hardest question. "Are you here to tell me it's over?"

She blinked. "No! Oh, Luke. No…"

He felt relief again—sweet relief. But he felt anger, too. Whatever she wouldn't tell him, it was big. He knew it had to be, or she wouldn't have let him go half the day without a word from her when she'd promised that she would get back to him; she wouldn't have ignored his calls.

He stepped away from her, turning.

She grabbed his arm. "Luke. Please. It's not about you. It's not about…us. Not really."

He shook off her grip. "Not really? What does that mean?"

"I'm only saying that it's a family matter."

"You're lying."

"No. No, I'm not. It *is* a family issue."

"And it's also about us. Isn't it?"

"Luke, it's not—"

He put up a hand. "I don't need to know what it's *not* about."

"I…yes. All right. Of course. I understand." She fell silent, her gaze down. And then she looked up at him, those black eyes begging. "I gave my word. Don't ask me to break my promise."

"Gave your word to who?"

She shut her eyes. "I can't say anymore. I *won't* say anymore." A shudder went through her. She stared down at the floor again, her hair falling forward like a black satin waterfall. "Do you…want me to go?"

The need to reach for her, to comfort her, was so powerful. He resisted it and asked flatly, "Do you want to go?"

"No." She said it so softly, her gaze still focused on the floor. "I want to stay here. With you."

"But you're not going to talk to me."

"I…no. I'm not. I can't. Not now."

He should tell her to go, get the hell out. And not to come back until she could reveal whatever secret she was keeping from him—or he should just drop it, let it alone. Trust her. Accept her word that it wasn't about the two of them. Let her keep her damn secret, tell him if and when she was ready.

Somehow, he could do neither. He couldn't bear to send her away. And he couldn't stand that something was really bothering her and she wouldn't tell him what.

"Look at me," he commanded. She raised her head again and met his eyes.

"Trust me, Luke." She whispered the words, echoing his thoughts of a moment before. "Please. Just trust me."

"I do trust you. But I don't believe you. Something's wrong. Very wrong. And it *is* about us."

"I'll go." She started to turn.

"Mercy."

She stopped, her hand on the crystal doorknob.

"Turn around."

Slowly, she faced him, raising her chin high, meeting his eyes, refusing now to look away.

"Take off your clothes."

She swallowed, licked her lips. A sigh trembled through her. And then she reached for the first button at the top of her shirt. Deftly, she undid those buttons, one after the other.

He should have been a little patient. He knew that. Should have taken her in his arms again, kissed her some more and spoken gently to her.

But he didn't *feel* gentle. Or patient. Or understanding. He felt that he was losing her, no matter that she said he wasn't. If she wouldn't talk to him, he needed to have her naked in his arms. He needed that now. There was some major barrier between them that she wouldn't even explain to him. He needed at least to feel her, to touch her, skin to skin.

As she undressed, he pulled his shirt up and off, jumped on one foot and then the other to get out of his boots. He ripped off his socks, tore down his zipper and yanked it wide. He skimmed off his Wranglers and his underwear, too.

They finished simultaneously. She was naked. He was naked. He reached for her and dragged her against him, fisting his hands in the lush silk of her hair, pulling her head back to take her mouth.

She didn't resist him. Her lips opened like the petals of a sun-warmed flower. He speared his tongue in, tasting her, claiming her. She moaned into his mouth, a sound of total surrender, and she pressed her body against him, all soft, womanly curves, smelling of sweetness and of spice.

Already, he was hard for her, needing her. So bad. Still kissing her, he tugged her backward, across the floor of the sitting room, into his bedroom, all the way to the side of the bed and the drawer in the nightstand where he kept the condoms. Never breaking his hungry kiss, he pulled the drawer open, got what he needed and shoved the drawer shut. One-handed, he tried to get the damn thing open, but it wasn't happening.

He growled his frustration into her mouth. And he felt her touch, her hand on his, gentle as a breath, taking the condom from him. They broke the never-ending kiss to look down together at her slim, deft fingers as she tore the wrapper free and smoothly rolled the protection down over his hard, aching length.

When it was on, she glanced up at him, her eyes low and lazy, soft with desire. "I love you, Luke. I am yours.

Always. No matter what happens. In my heart, I will always be yours. Believe that, if nothing else."

He did believe it. And he should have said it back to her—told her of his love. But his throat was thick with need, and with hurt at her refusal to speak openly. And with fear, too—that he was losing her. That somehow, he had already lost her. That this, now, the two of them, naked, together, was the ending of everything they'd shared.

Love.

No. He wouldn't—couldn't speak of it. The word was all wrong at a time like this. It was a salve, a gentle word and nothing more.

He cupped her breasts in his hands, so full, so perfectly formed, so exactly suited to his desire. And he caught the nipples, twisting them. Hurting her a little. She moaned, pressing her hips up to him, against his yearning hardness, her head falling back to reveal the silky skin of her throat. He lowered his mouth and latched on to the tight flesh, sucking hard enough to mark her, to leave a bruise.

She moaned again, her fingers in his hair, holding him hard against her. He kissed the place he'd sucked and he let his touch wander down along her ribcage and lower.

He molded the indentation of her waist, then traced the smooth swells of her hips, his hands moving lower still to grasp her bottom. He lifted her.

She knew what to do—she wrapped those long, strong legs around him, lifting that fraction higher, to position herself. He was at her entrance, easing his fingers between her spread thighs to test her readiness.

Wet. Silky. Hot.

He licked his way up her throat, until her mouth was

beneath his. And he claimed her again with a deep, seeking kiss.

"Luke…" She formed his name, even with his tongue in her mouth.

He surged up into her, then, hard and deep. She helped him, pressing down, groaning low as he filled her.

"Luke. Ah, Luke…"

He gripped her tightly against him and fell back across the bed, giving her the top position. She rose up above him, rocking her hips, riding him hard. He reached up to fill his hands with those full breasts of hers, to clasp her waist, to lay his palm flat on her belly and then ease his fingers lower.

She shuddered as he found the swollen center of her pleasure. He stroked it as she rode him, driving her higher, watching her face above him, her head thrown back, full lips softly parted, eyes closed in ecstasy.

Her soft woman's groan—a sound like a purr, deep and building to a frantic cry—warned him. And then, against his caressing fingers, he felt the flutter, like the wings of a night moth unfurling.

And then he was coming, too. He took her by the waist and pulled her down hard on him as his body surged up into hers, his seed spilling. She pulsed around him, all he'd every wanted, all he'd never known he needed.

The days and nights they'd shared played through him, like a sad, haunting song remembered, a time lost already, but never to be forgotten.

He saw her in the stable, eyes wide and wounded, lips red and swollen, after their first kiss. And at the cabin in the Hill Country, astride one of his mares, her hair wild in the wind, laughing. And in her bright kitchen at her little house, holding the roses he'd brought her, giving him a smile that could light up the night…

So many tender memories, strung together like diamonds, shining painfully bright, burned like a brand onto his heart.

Her body went lax above him. She collapsed against his chest, her face buried against his shoulder, her lips whispering, forming his name.

"Luke. I love you. I love you, I do."

"Shh." He stroked her hair, traced the perfect shell of her ear, wished that they could just stay like this forever, holding each other close, the sweat of their lovemaking drying on their naked bodies in the aftermath of shared pleasure.

But it wasn't to be.

She lifted up enough to rest her folded arms on his chest, to settle her chin on her hands. Her black hair fanned out, falling against his skin. He laced his fingers behind his head and she traced a heart on the pale flesh at the inside of his bicep.

"It will…work out," she whispered. "You'll see."

So why then, he wondered, did her eyes have shadows in them, why did they speak to him of suffering—and doubt?

"You're sure?" he asked, still not believing, but giving her the chance to be honest, at least.

She stretched up and kissed the cleft in his chin. "I am."

He sprung the trap. "Then how about I invite my family here to Bravo Ridge next weekend? A family dinner. You'll be my date."

She blinked. "I… You want me to, um, meet the parents, now?"

"Next Saturday. What do you say?"

"Well, I…I don't think that's the way to go about it."

"Not the way."

"No."

"All right, Mercy. What *is* the way, then?"

"Oh, well, a private talk, I think, with your parents, alone, just us and them, first of all."

"Fair enough. When will you be available for a private talk with my mom and dad?"

She pulled back then, sitting up and swinging her legs over the side of the bed, away from him, showing him the vulnerable curve of her sleek, bare back, her hair a tangled halo, darkness kissed with light. "Luke, I can't. Not now…" She spoke without turning.

"When?"

She hung her head. "I don't know."

Chapter Thirteen

It was no good. Mercy knew it. He wanted more than she could give right then. He wanted answers that she couldn't provide. It wasn't her place to share the secret her mother had revealed.

Not now, anyway. Maybe later. Who could know?

But right then, on that bleak Saturday evening, as dusk began to darken the corners of his bedroom, she simply couldn't. She was duty-bound to let her mother, her sister and her poor, betrayed father— wherever he was now—figure out what *they* wanted to do first.

He was silent behind her. Really, what more was there to say? He had tried over and over to get her to open up to him. She couldn't blame him for deciding he'd tried hard enough.

She rose from the bed and put her clothes on, turning

to him again only when she was fully dressed. He had been watching her.

But when she looked at him, he rolled his golden head away.

So she left him there, naked in the growing darkness, on the tangled blankets of the bed where they had made love. As she drove home, she wondered if she would ever see him again.

It hurt so bad to think that.

She couldn't bear it. Her heart leapt instantly into denials. It was a bad time, that was all. He was hurt and angry with her, but time would heal the rift. What they shared was too powerful to die because of a single secret she felt honor-bound to keep from him.

But ah, *Dios,* what a secret. The kind that, revealed, could damage his family as badly as it had hers.

She stopped at her mother's house before she went home.

Luz was there, dry-eyed, alone. She said that Elena had called. "To check on me, to make certain I haven't added suicide to all my other sins. I told her I was all right and she didn't need to worry. And then I said I loved her—before I realized that she'd already hung up."

"Give her time, *Mami.*" The words sounded empty to Mercy's ears. *Give her time, give* it *time.* It seemed to be the only answer she had now.

Her mother smiled the saddest smile. "I don't think I have any choice, *mija*—what's that on your neck?"

Mercy touched the place where Luke had kissed her, a small, hot shiver running through her at the memory. She really should have thought to cover it. But too late now. She looked at her mother levelly.

And Luz waved a hand. "It's one good thing out of all this pain and shame. That I can wish only the best for you now. May your love give you joy, Mercy. Sometimes God works in strange and wonderful ways."

Mercy looked away. If her mother found comfort in religion, well, that was all to the good. "We can hope."

She told her mother about the note her dad had left. Luz only shook her head and whispered something low in Spanish.

"He said he was safe and well, Mom."

"Okay, then. That's something. For now, I think it's the best I can hope for."

Mercy didn't reply. What could she say? She could see no way that her proud father could ever forgive her mother's betrayal.

At home, she found Elena in pajamas on the sofa, a take-out pizza on the coffee table and Orlando in her lap.

Elena tossed a half-eaten slice back into the box. "What are you doing back so early?" she asked—and then she understood. "Ah, *chica. Lo siento...*"

"Don't be sorry. It's not your fault. He's angry with me. I don't blame him. It seemed kind of pointless to stay." She'd put makeup on the love-bruise, but Elena had sharp eyes. Mercy caught her looking at it. Elena smiled, but didn't say anything. Mercy asked, "You got enough pizza for two?"

"I got an extra large. Plenty for both of us."

So Mercy put on her pj's and they had pizza and Pepsi.

"I stopped in at Mom's on the way back from Bravo Ridge," Mercy said. "She told me you had called her."

"I said I would—and can we not talk about her?"

"Just…letting you know what happened."

A moment or two of silence and then Elena said softly, "I called Dad, too." Mercy sent her a questioning look. Elena shrugged. "Straight to voice mail."

Mercy opened her mouth to reply, but shut it when she realized she was about to say, *Give it time.*

Sunday, Mercy was on call again. She delivered a breech-born colt and stitched up a pair of calves that'd had run-ins with a mean length of barbed-wire fence. Late in the afternoon, she worked at the clinic. The small-animal vet who usually handled weekends needed some time off. Mercy performed two minor surgeries and saved the life of a German shepherd that had been hit by a car.

She didn't get home until after eight. Elena had made their mother's secret recipe for chili verde burritos and waited to eat until Mercy got there. She had the kitchen table set for two.

The food was delicious, though it brought back memories of the four of them around the table at the small house not far from Mercy's place, where they had grown up; of their father's deep laughter and their mother's warm smiles. Of the glances of love and happiness they would share across the table…

Elena had tears in her eyes. She waved a hand. "Too many jalapeños, I think…"

Mercy only nodded.

Monday was uneventful. Mercy worked with one ear on her cell, hoping Luke might call. He never did.

At night, she took the heart-shaped rock—the one she'd found at the cabin the first time he took her there—to bed with her. She held it in her hand all night, her own personal worry stone.

She longed to call him. But somehow, it didn't seem her place to make the first move. Not until she was willing to talk to him, to tell him everything Elena had asked her not to say.

Tuesday was the same. She waited to hear from him, but he didn't call. Neither did her dad. Elena asked her to try Javier's cell again, reasoning that maybe he would pick up for Mercy. Again, without a single ring, she got voice mail. She left a message asking him, please, to call and tell them that he was all right.

An hour later, Marcella called. Javier had called *her* and asked her to tell his daughters to stop worrying.

"He couldn't just answer and tell us that?" Elena muttered with a snort of disgust.

"Guess not," Mercy said softly.

"After a little longer of this, I could get to hate him."

"Don't say things you don't mean. We should probably check on Mom, too."

"You do it."

"I think I should go over there."

"Hey. Go for it."

Mercy's mom wasn't at home. She tried her cell. Luz answered on the first ring. "I'm at the office. It's good to keep busy in difficult times."

"Call, *Mami*. If you need me."

"I will. Take care of your sister."

"I promise."

Wednesday dragged by. And Thursday, too. By Thursday evening, Mercy was considering calling Luke and telling him the truth, no matter the consequences.

It was just too painful to continue like this. And not only because going on like this had her wondering if she had lost him. There was also the powerful feeling that she'd betrayed him somehow—by not trusting him enough, by lying straight to his face, insisting that her secret had nothing to do with them, with their love.

When it did. It had everything to do with them. It was about the families they cherished.

She saw, the more she turned her own suffering over in her mind and heart, that in a way, she had been protecting him. She didn't want him to have to face the truth about his own father's betrayal of his mother, didn't want him to see the cracks in the foundation on which he had built his life and his beliefs, didn't want him to suffer as she and Elena—and their mother and father—were suffering.

She still didn't want him to suffer. But she was beginning to see that it wasn't her place to protect him, to make that call for him when he had insisted that what he wanted from her, above all, was honesty.

As it turned out, he called her—that night, while she and Elena were eating dinner. She got up and answered the phone and the sound of his voice nearly doubled her over with longing, with love.

"Come to the cabin with me tomorrow?" he asked.

She breathed her heartfelt, "Yes," before he'd finished the question.

A low chuckle escaped him. "You don't have to play hard to get with me."

"Good. Because I'm not."

"I'll pick you up at your place. Six o'clock?"

"I'll be ready."

"Okay, then." And he was gone.

She hung up slowly, feeling strangely reverent, her body, head-to-toe, aglow with pure happiness.

"About time he called." Elena picked up her water glass and took a sip. The ice cubes clinked as she set it back down.

Mercy returned to the table, lowering herself slowly, feeling fragile and joyful, both at the same time. "He's taking me to the cabin this weekend."

"Good. You could use a nice getaway. Forget all your problems for a change."

"Will you be okay while I'm gone?"

"Yes, I will. Don't worry about me."

"You're certain?"

"Mercy, what did I say?"

Mercy rested her hands on either side of her plate and stared blindly down at her food, trying to put the right words to what she needed to say.

Elena noticed her struggle. "What? Go ahead, say it."

Mercy faced her sister. "I have to tell him what's happened. I'm *going* to tell him."

Elena gasped, but she didn't speak. Not right away. Finally, she nodded. "He's an honorable man, I think."

"Yes, he is."

"I had hoped to wait a little, to see if *Papi*..." The words trailed off. She shook her head. "Could I ask you one thing?"

"Anything. You know that."

"You're sure he needs to know?"

"Elena, he knows I'm hiding something important from him. He hates it. He believes I don't trust him. Either I end it with him or I get straight."

"Yes. All right. I can see that. But if he has to know, well, does he have to tell anyone?"

"You don't want Davis Bravo to know that he's your father."

"Because he's *not* my father." There was passion in her voice now. Real heat. "He's…a sperm donor, that's all. My father is Javier Cabrera and I don't want him hurt any more than he's already been. I want to at least talk with him, with *Papi,* before anyone confronts Davis Bravo with the results of his own betrayal."

It seemed a reasonable request. No, Mercy didn't want to put conditions on being truthful with Luke. But in this case, she couldn't deny her sister's plea. "Fair enough. I'll get Luke's word before I tell him. I'll get his promise to tell no one else."

"Ay." Elena rubbed her temples, as if a headache pounded there. "It's all so twisted, isn't it? So ugly and sad."

"We will get through this somehow."

Elena dropped her hands to her lap. "Yeah. You're right. I know we will."

Elena was at the house when Luke arrived the next day. She walked Mercy out to his fancy pickup, which he'd parked at the curb. Like the last time they went to the cabin, he was pulling a two-horse trailer.

He got out and put Mercy's suitcase in back. Then he greeted Elena in a friendly way, avoiding dangerous subjects like why she'd broken her date with his brother, sticking to the usual hi-how-are-you stuff.

Orlando had followed them out. He sat on the sidewalk,

panting, looking hopeful he would be taken along. Lollie waited in the rear of the cab, making eager little moans.

"Well," said Luke. "Put Orlando in back and we're out of here."

Mercy shared a glance with her sister. Elena had already asked if he might stay with her. "He's staying, keeping Elena company." She bent to hug the dog goodbye and then hugged her sister, too. "Don't hesitate to call, if there's anything…"

Elena took her by the shoulders and gently pushed her away. "I'll be fine. Go. Bye, Luke."

He tipped his hat to her and held the door for Mercy. She got in and buckled up. He went around and got in, too. They shared a glance. She saw a hundred questions in his eyes.

But he didn't ask them. He started the engine and they drove away.

At the cabin, they let the horses loose in the paddock out back. They took their things inside and put them away for the weekend. Then they wandered into the kitchen, where Luke filled Lollie's water bowl and gave her some food.

"Hungry?" He went to the fridge and opened the door. As before, it was packed with everything they might possibly want to eat during the weekend to come.

She touched his arm. "Luke…"

He turned to her, blue eyes tender. And sad, too. "I haven't asked a single question."

"No. You haven't."

He tipped her chin up with a finger. And then his lips settled on hers in a kiss so sweet it made an ache within her, a yearning too beautiful for words. He wrapped her close in his arms, whispered into her hair, "God. I've missed you. So damn much…"

"I know. Me, too."

His palm glided down her arm and he caught her hand in his. "Come on."

She went with him into the bedroom, where the covers were turned back, the white sheets so inviting. She thought of all the things she was going to tell him, even considered saying them now, right away.

But no. It was too perfect a moment. He asked nothing but to hold her, to bring her pleasure and fulfillment. And his hands on her body, his lips pressed to hers… yes. Oh, yes. Right now, that was enough.

They made slow, sweet love as the day faded to night.

And then they rose. He put on a soft pair of old sweatpants and she her short silk robe. They went out to the kitchen to fry a fat pair of pork chops and heat up the garlic mashed potatoes the caretaker's wife had left for them.

Luke opened a bottle of wine, but Mercy shook her head when he offered to fill her glass. Lately, alcohol didn't agree with her. It was probably all the tension in the past week. In fact, all at once, her stomach felt queasy.

Having to tell a terrible truth will do that to a person.

He raised his glass and she raised her water goblet. "To us," he said.

She sipped and set down her glass and picked up her fork—and knew that if she didn't tell him now, she would find a way to avoid doing it. He seemed to have accepted her terms of silence. Of not talking about what both of them were thinking. It was so tempting, just to say nothing.

Her stomach rolled. She swallowed hard and breathed

in through her nose. "This won't work," she said. And she held his eyes. "Will it?"

He set down his wineglass. "I'm trying."

"I know. And I love you for it, more, if possible, than before."

"But?"

"You know and I know. I *am* keeping something from you. Something important."

He studied her face, so intently, as if he could read the truth there. "And you've decided to tell me?"

"I have." She watched his face brighten. "Don't look so happy. You won't be, once you know."

He scowled then. "Mercy, damn you. You're driving me crazy. What?"

She sipped more water to try and calm her still-churning stomach. "I...I promised someone I would get your word first, that what I tell you, you can't tell anyone else."

He swore, rising and shoving back his chair so hard it tipped over behind him and crashed to the floor. In the corner, Lollie jumped and let out a whine. He tossed his napkin on the table and turned from her. She stared at his beautiful, muscular back. And she wanted to rise, to go to him, to wrap her arms around him and promise him...

What? She had nothing to promise him but a truth that would only hurt him.

So she made herself keep silent. She made herself wait, breathing in and out carefully through her nose, ordering her strange nausea to pass.

At last, he turned to her again. His blue eyes looked so dark then, dark as the deepest part of the night. "Okay. You have my promise. Whatever you tell me, I'll keep to myself." He bent and righted the chair, but he didn't sit. He kept hold of the back of it in a white-knuckled grip. "Talk. Now."

Her heart knocking away like jungle drums, sure that any second she would throw up, she asked, "You remember, years ago, that my mother worked for your father?"

"Yeah. So?"

"Well, they, um, had an affair."

He swore again. An uglier word than the ones before. "No."

"Yes. Yes, it's true. They had an affair, your father and my mother. A three-week affair. They both felt terrible about it. There were problems in both of their marriages at the time, but your dad still loved your mother and my mom loved my dad. They broke it off. And then they realized they couldn't work together. So they decided she would quit, and they would say he had fired her so that she could get unemployment to tide her over till she found something else." Mercy made herself keep looking at him. Looking right into his eyes. It wasn't easy.

He was furious. "Who told you this?"

"My mother."

"She's lying."

"No, she's not. And there's more."

"What the hell? What more could there...?" He figured it out, right then. He knew. She saw it in his eyes, the fury fading, replaced by a horrified wonder, as he put it together: *His* father calling *her* mother when he found out about the two of them; her sister saying yes to Caleb—and then calling him back and saying no. "Elena."

She nodded. "She's your half sister. Davis is her biological father."

A stark, awful silence. Then, "My father, does he…?"

"He doesn't know, Luke." She pressed her hand to her stomach, hoping the touch might soothe its roiling. "My mother never told him. And she never told my father, either. Until last Saturday—when Caleb asked my sister out and my mother's guilt and shame finally drove her to blow the lie wide-open…until then, my dad believed that Elena was his."

He yanked the chair back and dropped into it, hard. After a minute, he scrubbed his hands down his face. And then, finally, he looked at her again. "I get now why you didn't want to tell me."

Softly she asked, "And do you wish I hadn't?"

His gaze didn't waver. "No. I needed to know. That's why Elena's staying at your house?"

"Yes. She won't stay with my mother and her own place isn't ready for a couple of weeks."

"Your mother and father?"

"Mom's okay, considering. I kind of think it's a relief, in a way, for her to finally be done with living a lie."

"Your dad?"

"He left. We don't know where he went. He wrote me a note, to say he's okay, but he needs some time away. And, well, that's why Elena asked me to get your word that you would keep quiet about this. She needs to talk to him before she decides what to do next."

"I don't like it, not any of it."

"I didn't think you would. It's one of the reasons I didn't want to tell you."

"There was no hiding it from me, you know that, don't you?" His eyes held tenderness now. "You're a really bad liar, Mercy."

She looked across at him, still holding her queasy stomach, loving him so completely, at the same time as she wondered how she could hold so much sadness in her aching heart. "It's strange, if you think about it. They say the truth will set you free. But it doesn't, does it? It only binds you tighter than before."

Bound.

Luke watched Mercy's face across the table and thought that there had never in all time been such a woman. So brave and good and loyal. And so damn beautiful, it broke a man's heart just to look at her.

Bound. He was bound to her. Tied up tight as a roped calf. He would never escape her. She held his heart.

But that was all right. He didn't want to escape her. He wanted...a life with her. A family. With her.

He knew that what he wanted was forbidden—especially now, given what she'd just told him. She'd handed over yet more proof of the old adage that Bravos and Cabreras should never mix.

His father, her mother. It didn't seem possible.

And Elena his half sister...

What a hopeless mess.

Only one thing was clear: Mercy. Across the table from him, her face full of sadness. And love.

They *were* bound, the two of them. Bound in a good way. The best way. By love, deep and true. And the ongoing folly of their families could not be allowed to keep them apart.

Not anymore. Not a damn minute longer.

He rose from his chair again, but this time more carefully, pushing it back, slowly getting to his feet.

"Luke?" Mercy stared up at him, her mouth a soft O. Something in his face must have surprised her.

He took the steps that would bring him to her chair, not knowing, really, what he meant to do until he got there.

"Luke. What?" Her eyes shone up at him, black as ebony, endlessly deep. She had her hand on her stomach, which was kind of strange, but she shifted toward him, moving her smooth bare legs from under the table.

He sank on one knee. "Mercy…" He reached for the hand that wasn't pressed to her belly. Numbly, she gave it. He kissed her fingers.

She asked, "Luke, what's happening?"

He raised his head to look at her, laying his free hand on top of hers, so it was captured between his two palms. "Mercy." His throat clutched. He had to whisper the words. "Marry me."

She let out a cry. And then she shoved him away.

He fell backward. "Mercy, what the hell?"

But she was already up on her feet, her hand over her mouth, taking off at a run.

Chapter Fourteen

Mercy skidded into the bathroom, flung herself to the floor by the toilet and threw back the lid—just in time.

She gagged, hard. The contents of her stomach spewed into the toilet bowl. She groaned. And it happened again. And again.

A warm hand pressed lightly at her back. "Easy. It's okay…" Luke. The poor man. She reached up and dragged on the flush lever, then moaned again and closed her eyes as the fouled water whirled inside the bowl.

She heard water running in the sink. Luke knelt beside her, offering a cool, wet cloth. She took it from him and wiped her face. Then she shut the toilet lid and leaned her cheek against it, waiting.

Nothing. Her stomach had stopped churning. She felt empty. And so tired.

Also, her mouth tasted like something had died in there. "Ugh." She groaned. "I need a toothbrush..."

"Come on, then." He was so sweet and gentle with her. He helped her up and got her toothbrush and toothpaste. He squeezed a glob of paste on the brush and handed it to her.

She made a face as she took it. "Sure you don't want to brush for me, too?"

He smoothed her hair out of her eyes. "Anything you need. Just say it."

She gave him a long glance, thinking what a wonderful man he was. And then she turned to the sink and stuck the toothbrush in her mouth.

Her face, in the mirror above the faucet, looked slightly green. When she finished brushing, she rinsed her mouth and the brush, and then put the brush away. "I can't believe I just hurled when you asked me to marry you."

He chuckled and touched the back of his finger to her cheek. "It wasn't the reaction I was hoping for, I have to admit—and you look like you need to lie down."

"Great idea."

He scooped her up against his chest and carried her to the bedroom, where he lowered her gently to the bed.

She patted the mattress and he sat down beside her. "Marriage." She said the word softly. It made her feel reverent. And scared, too. "Oh, Luke..."

He bent, brushed his lips to hers. "Consider it. Will you do that, just think about it?"

"Oh, yes. It's *all* I'll think about—I mean, other than the whole big family problem."

"I know it must seem like the worst possible time to

talk about getting married. But we have to ask ourselves, will there ever be a *good* time?"

She sighed. "Probably not."

He pulled the sheet up from the bottom of the bed and smoothed it over her. "You're the woman for me, Mercy. I think I've known it forever, since the first time I looked in those eyes of yours when you were twelve years old. And if that's too ridiculous and hopelessly romantic, well, I've loved you at least since that first time I kissed you, in the stable, when you came to sew up my prize stallion's torn ear."

She reached up, touched his lips. They were soft. Warm. The lips she wanted to kiss. Always. For the rest of her life. "I will never forget that night."

He caught her hand, kissed the pads of her fingers. "I have to ask."

"What?"

"Are you pregnant?"

She gaped at him. Such a thought had never occurred to her. "I…well, I don't know."

"You just threw up."

"Well, yeah. I know."

"Do you do that often, out of nowhere like that?"

"Of course not. I…" She put her hand on her belly. Was it possible? "We did forget the condom, didn't we, that first weekend?"

"Is your period late?"

"I couldn't say. I've been so irregular since I cut out the pill last time." She'd visited her doctor a few weeks before and gotten another prescription. "As a matter of fact, I've been waiting to *have* a period, so I can start taking the pills again."

"Say you got pregnant that first time, when we messed up…"

"Yeah?"

"Could you take a test now, and find out?"

"Well, I…if I *am* pregnant, that would mean my period is actually late, right?"

He blinked. "You're asking *me?* I know squat about this."

"I'm only saying that I think, with the home tests, you can use them the first day of a missed period. Some of them may even work sooner nowadays. I'm not sure, though. I'm only going from the magazine ads. It's not as I've ever had to use one.…"

He looked so handsome and so befuddled, both at the same time. "Is that a yes? Could you take a test now— *would* you take a test now?"

"I, well, I…" She felt dizzy at the very idea. A baby. Could she be pregnant? Well, of course she could. It *was* possible. It just seemed like one too many giant issues to stew about. Didn't they have enough to deal with already?

And he was watching her, looking so worried, waiting for her to give him an answer.

"Yes," she said breathlessly. "Yes, of course. I could. I would."

"Tomorrow, then." He was practically whispering. As if the two of them shared some enormous, scary secret—which she supposed they did. "We'll go into Fredericksburg first thing and buy a test."

That night, Mercy lay awake, staring at the ceiling. Thinking about marrying Luke. About having his baby.

About having Davis Bravo for a father-in-law. Never in her life would she have guessed she'd be considering marriage to one of Davis Bravo's sons.

But that was just it. He was Luke first—*her* Luke. And somehow, the longer she knew him, the less she thought of him as her enemy's son.

And if there was a baby…

Ah, *Dios*. What would she say to her poor *papi?* How could she tell him? He'd been hurt so much already.

"You could look at it as a way to finally start putting an end to almost sixty years of pointless hatred." Luke's voice came to her, soft and thoughtful in the quiet darkness of the bedroom.

She found his hand under the covers, wove her fingers with his. "Did you just read my mind?"

He chuckled softly. "I don't need mystical powers to guess why you're still awake."

"I'm so scared, Luke. And worried. About my Dad, especially."

"I know." He turned toward her.

She went into his embrace, snuggling up close, sighing in contentment at the feel of his arms around her. He smelled of soap and man and a hint of aftershave. If she left him, how would she live without the scent of him, without the warmth of his body enfolding hers? She couldn't. She wouldn't. "I can't imagine my life without you now."

"I know the feeling."

"It would have to be like a sacred trust, I think. We would have to commit ourselves not only to each other, but to the healing of our families."

"And to the baby, too."

"That goes without saying. The baby, too. I mean, *if* there really is a baby…"

He stroked the side of her neck, fingers trailing out to caress the curve of her shoulder. "I'm willing."

"Elena and Caleb would be with us from the first. And my mother, too, I think?"

"Your mother?" He sounded doubtful.

She nodded against his chest, pressing her lips there, above the place where his heart beat. "Last Saturday, after I left you, I went to check on her. She saw that hickey you gave me."

He chuckled. "Sorry 'bout that."

She kissed his chest again. "No, you're not."

"Well, I *was* afraid I was losing you…."

"You marked me as yours."

"Okay, yeah. I did."

"And my mother saw it. She said she hoped my love gave me happiness. That God sometimes works in mysterious ways. I played it off when she said it. But tonight, I keep thinking about it."

He lifted her chin with a finger. "Sometimes you think too much."

She saw the gleam in his eyes. "I know what *you're* thinking."

His white teeth flashed as he grinned. "Well, as long as we're both awake…"

In the morning, they drove into Fredericksburg for breakfast. Mercy hardly touched her food. She was too keyed up, wondering whether or not she was pregnant. They stopped in at a Walgreens before heading back to the cabin.

At the cabin, they read the instructions. Mercy went into the bathroom and peed on the stick.

She carried the results out to him.

"Well?" His blue eyes were very wide.

Suddenly, her stomach was churning again. "I couldn't do it."

"Couldn't do what?"

"I couldn't look. Here. You do it." She shoved it at him.

He took it from her. "Two blue lines."

"Omigod."

"We're having a baby, Mercy."

"Omigod."

"Mercy." He ripped a Kleenex from the box on the nightstand and set the testing stick on it. Then he reached for her. And all at once, she was laughing, her nausea gone as swiftly as it had come. He lifted her high and swung her around. She braced her hands on his broad shoulders and let her head fall back and her laugh of pure joy ring out.

And then he slowed his spinning. He stopped with his feet braced wide and let her slide down the length of him.

She whispered looking up into his eyes, "It's a big step."

He commanded, "Marry me."

"Yes," she answered, certain at last of what she wanted—of what was right. "Oh, Luke. Yes!"

Elena's car was in the driveway Sunday when Luke dropped Mercy off. He offered to come in with her, but she shook her head.

"There's so much to tell her. I'd rather do it on my own. It's a sister thing."

"You're not going to back out on me, are you?"

"No way. Never again. We're getting married. It's settled."

He kissed her. Hard. "Tomorrow night?"

"I'll come to you as soon as I'm done working," she vowed.

"I'll be waiting."

They shared yet another kiss. And then she got out and got her bag and waved goodbye as he drove off.

Elena was waiting just inside the door. "Well? Did you have a good time?"

"The best."

Orlando was there beside Elena, waiting for some love. Mercy bent and scratched him thoroughly behind both ears. Then she jumped up and grabbed her sister in a bear hug.

"Whoa," cried Elena. "I guess it must have been good."

"Oh, most definitely." She led Elena to the sofa, sat her down, and told her everything, all in a rush.

Elena was speechless. But not for long. "*Tía* Elena. I like the sound of that." She let out a squeal of joy and grabbed Mercy for another orgy of hugging and happy cries.

When they settled down a little, Mercy said, "The wedding will be soon. In the next few weeks. And small. Just the families if we can get them to swear they won't kill each other. Friday, Luke's having his parents out to the ranch and we'll tell them—not about Mom and Davis. Not…your secret. That's for you to do, when you're ready. And not about the baby. Not yet. But that we love each other and we're getting married right away."

Elena's lips curved in a sad smile. "And what about *Mami* and *Papi?*"

"I'll tell her tomorrow about the wedding. You'll be my maid of honor?"

"You know I will. But *Papi*...?"

Mercy took both her sister's hands. "I hate that he's suffering. I do. But I'm starting to get a little mad at him, too."

"Yeah," Elena admitted. "So am I. It's been over a week. It's not *our* fault, what Mom did. He could *talk* to us, at least."

"My thoughts, exactly. I *am* going to try to find him and ask him if he would consider putting aside his bitterness and pain for a day to give me away. But I've made my choice to be with Luke. It wasn't an easy choice. I owe Mom and Dad so much. I don't want to hurt them..."

Elena finished for her. "But it's right." She spoke with reverence. "You and Luke, loving each other. That's about the rightest thing that's happened around here lately."

Mercy called her mom and asked her to meet her for lunch the next day. And then she called Luke. He said he'd set it up with Aleta. They were on for Friday night.

"Nervous?" he asked.

"Scared to death. But determined. And so much in love—with you."

He made a sound of satisfaction low in his throat. "You're amazing, you know that?"

"See you after work tomorrow."

He said he loved her and they hung up. She spent the evening with Elena. They planned the simple wedding.

It would be at Bravo Ridge and there would be a justice of the peace. Later, when things were better with the families, Mercy hoped she and Luke might have another ceremony with Father Francis presiding in the Catholic Church.

The next day, when Mercy told her mother that she and Luke were getting married, Luz reached across the table to cover Mercy's hand with hers.

"Be happy, *mija*."

Mercy breathed a slow sigh. "I wasn't sure how you would take it."

"I've had a lot to learn," Luz said softly. "And a terrible wrong to make right. I may never succeed at that. But at least I can live honestly now. At least I can give you my blessing, such as it is, to be with the one that you love."

Monday, Luke asked Zita to set the table in the kitchen for two and have the food ready by six.

Mercy didn't get there until after seven. When she arrived, he was waiting on the veranda. She wore jeans and a T-shirt, her hair pulled back the way she wore it when she was working. He wanted to sweep her into his arms and carry her off to his rooms and make wild love to her, dinner be damned. But she needed her nourishment, especially now, with the baby coming.

The baby.

He'd always wanted a big family like the one he'd grown up in. Hard to believe he was finally getting started on that. With Mercy.

Except for the family feud crap, life couldn't be better.

He kissed her slow and deep right there on the

veranda and then led her inside and back to the kitchen. "Pot roast and red potatoes," he announced as he held her chair for her.

She sat and smoothed her napkin on her lap. "Smells great and I'm starving."

He waited on her, dishing up the food, pouring her a tall, cold glass of milk. When he sat down opposite her, they grinned across the table at each other. He thought of all the years to come, when they would sit down at the table together, just like tonight. Damn. Life could be tough. But it was also good. Real good.

She'd just toasted him with her glass of milk, when they heard footsteps coming from the front of the house. Mercy set down her glass.

His mother appeared in the doorway.

Shocked the hell out of Luke. "Mom?" he asked stupidly.

She had a thick gauze bandage wrapped around her upper arm and a strange look in her deep blue eyes. "Sorry to intrude. It's only…" She sent a puzzled look at Mercy, who was sitting totally still. "Hello."

So much for waiting until Friday night to break the big news. "Mom. This is Mercy Cabrera."

Aleta blinked three times in rapid succession. "Mercedes?"

Mercy pasted on a smile. "Hello, Mrs. Bravo."

"The, um, adopted one?" It was such an abrupt thing to say, and borderline rude. Aleta Bravo was never, ever rude. And rarely abrupt.

Mercy pushed back her chair. She didn't lose her smile. "Yes. That's right. I'm adopted." Luke stood, too. Mercy started toward his mother, her hand outstretched.

But before she got there, his mother's eyes rolled back in her head and she dropped to the floor in a dead faint.

"Sweet God," Mercy cried. They both rushed to her and knelt on either side of her limp body. Mercy checked her pulse. "Strong and even. Still, you'd better call an ambulance."

"Gotcha." He dug his cell from his pocket.

Right then, his mother opened her eyes. "Luke," she said sharply. "What are you doing?"

"Getting you an ambulance."

"Don't," she commanded, reaching up and snatching the phone from him before he could punch the call through. "I don't need an ambulance. I've had several shocks in a row, that's all. Other than that, I'm perfectly well."

"Like hell. What's that bandage on your arm?"

She frowned as she glanced at it. "Oh, this. I'll explain it all in a minute, I promise." She handed him back the phone. "Put that away. And help me up, please."

"I don't know if you ought to be moved."

She popped to sitting position. "I said, help me up."

Still doubtful, he did as she commanded. Mercy took one side and he took the other and they helped her to the table. She staggered a little in her expensive high heels, but she made it to the chair and sank into it with a sigh, then gazed up Mercy with a forced smile. "I do apologize. For asking rude questions. Not to mention for fainting dead away."

"It's all right," Mercy reassured her. "I'm sure you weren't expecting to see me here."

"Water?" Luke set the glass in front of her.

She drank half of it. "There." She set the glass down carefully. "Much better."

Luke reclaimed his chair and Mercy went and sat down again, too. For a few moments, they were silent. Nobody seemed to know what to say.

Finally, Luke asked, "Are you sure you're okay?"

His mother cleared her throat. "Absolutely."

"Then would you mind telling us what's going on?"

She cast a weak glance at Mercy. "Please. I would like to understand. Are the two of you…?"

Luke said, "I love Mercy. She loves me. We're getting married. The plan was to break it to you gently this weekend, but it doesn't seem to be working out that way."

"Oh. Well." Aleta pressed her slim, well-manicured hand to her chest and gave Mercy a wobbly smile. "I hope you will be very happy."

"Thank you."

Aleta drank the rest of her water and then asked Luke, "Does…your father know anything about this— about you and Mercedes?"

"Yeah. He had Zita and the Hoffmans spying on us. The night of Mary's birthday party, he tried to talk me into breaking it off."

Aleta pressed her lips together. "I knew there was something the past few weeks. He denied it, lied to my face. He has a lot to answer for, your father."

"Mom."

"Yes?"

"Something's happened. What?"

She put her palm against her forehead. "I simply don't know where to begin."

"Just…start anywhere. It doesn't matter."

She turned to Mercy. "Before I say anything, I want you to know that your father is okay. He's unharmed. And I swear to you, no charges will be brought against him. I will personally see to that."

Mercy gaped. "But...what happened?"

Aleta turned to him again. "I've left your father. I'm going to be staying here for a while."

"For God's sake, Mom. Talk."

"Yes. All right. Javier Cabrera came to our house this evening. He had a gun."

Chapter Fifteen

Mercy cried out—and then slapped a hand over her mouth to still the sound. Luke started to jump up, to go to her.

She shook her head. "No. Please. I didn't mean to scare you. I'm…all right, really."

"You sure?" He wanted to go to her as much for himself as for her. He needed her touch right then.

Did she see that in his eyes? Whether she did or not, she reached across the table. He met her halfway.

Once he had her hand in his, he said to his mother, "Go on."

She looked from his face to Mercy's and then back to him again. "Well." Her voice was whisper-soft. "I'm glad to see that you…" The words faded off. She regrouped and tried again. "It's clear, I mean, that you truly care for each other."

He gave her a nod. "Please. We have to know the rest."

"Of course." She took a slow breath through her nose. And then, at last, she told them. "Davis was home from the office when Javier arrived. We were in the front room, your father and I, having a drink before deciding where to go for dinner. There was a knock at the door. Since Linda had already gone home for the evening, I went to answer it.

"It was Javier. He had a pistol. A little silver thing. It almost looked like a toy. But it wasn't. I...stared at him, not understanding. He made a motion with the gun. He asked for Davis. And that was when Davis came in from the living room, wanting to know who it was. He saw. He said for me to get out of the way. And I...I did. Javier pointed the gun at Davis's heart. I didn't understand. It seemed so unreal.

"He started accusing Davis of...of having sex with his wife, of being the father of his daughter, Elena. It was all very confusing. I didn't really know at that moment what he was telling us. I saw he would shoot. I cried, 'No!' and I stepped in front of the gun. It went off. For such a small weapon, it was so terribly loud. I think Javier must have seen what I was doing, protecting my husband, and tried to turn the gun away at the last moment. Or maybe he realized that murder wasn't a good idea, no matter what Davis had done. Or maybe he just aimed poorly..."

"My dad shot you," Mercy murmured in horror.

"The bullet only grazed me." His mother spoke firmly. "I felt the burning along the outside of my arm. And then he—Javier—dropped the gun. He said he was sorry, that he shouldn't have done it, that he had done everything wrong. And then he turned and ran. Davis was all over me, then, checking to make certain I wasn't hurt too badly. When he saw I was barely grazed, he started after Javier.

"I grabbed him. I told him he was going nowhere, that I had a few questions for him and he'd better not tell me any more lies. I shut the door. I ordered him to get the first-aid kit. And while he bandaged my arm, I made him tell me, I made him confess."

"How terrible for you," Mercy whispered.

She turned to Mercy, her eyes full of pain. "I had known that there was an affair, all those years ago. Davis tried to deny it then. But I could see his guilt. And I had smelled another woman's perfume on him more than once. Finally, he confessed that there had been 'someone,' but that it was over. He insisted that I didn't need to know her name. I almost divorced him then, twenty-three years ago. But we worked it out, finally. Or I thought we had. Tonight, when he admitted that the woman he'd been with was Luz, he swore he didn't know there had been a child."

Mercy said gently, "Truly, I don't think he did know."

His mother frowned at her. "Why ever not?"

"My mother told me that she never told your husband. That she never told a soul. She convinced my father the baby was his, and that Elena had been born two months early."

"My God. The poor man." Aleta sat straighter in the chair. "Well, Davis has told way too many lies for me to believe anything he says now. Even if your mother never told him, it's still possible that he knew." She turned her gaze on Luke. "You know how he is. He keeps track of everything. I'm betting he would have known that Luz had a baby seven months after they had an affair."

"You can't be sure," he said gently. "Maybe you ought to give him the benefit of the doubt on that one."

She muttered, "He doesn't deserve the benefit of the doubt."

Mercy stood. "I'm sorry, but I really think I have to try and find my dad...." Right then, a cell phone started ringing—it was Mercy's, in her purse on the end of the counter. She hustled over there and answered it, checking the display and mouthing "It's Elena," to him, before she spoke into the phone. "Hi...yes." Her face went white. Luke lurched to his feet, but she put up a hand to hold him off. "Of course," she said into the phone. "Right away. Is he...?" She nodded, frantically. "Yes. Keep him there. I'm on my way." She flipped the phone shut. "My dad's at my house. I have to go."

"I'll go with you."

She shook her head. "No, Luke. I need to go on my own." She came to him. He pulled her close, wanting to hold on tight and never let go. She whispered, "Trust me. Please." Those dark eyes begged for his understanding.

What else could he do? "You're sure?"

"I am. Stay here with your mom. She needs you now."

"No." Aleta piped up from back at the table. "Really. I'm fine on my own. You should go with—"

"Shh, Mom..." Luke had eyes only for Mercy. She lifted her mouth. He kissed her, deeply.

Too quickly, she was pulling away. Grabbing her purse from the counter, she disappeared through the door to the hall.

Aleta said softly, "So, then. True love, is it?"

Luke stared at the empty doorway. "Yeah, Mom. True love."

Outside, it was growing dark. Mercy turned on her headlights and drove home as fast as she dared.

When she pulled onto her street, she saw her father's Cadillac pulling out of her driveway, fast. He pointed it the other way and hit the gas.

"No!" she cried, as if he could hear her.

She followed him, her stomach suddenly churning as she speeded past her house, where Elena stood on the porch, her arms wrapped around herself, Orlando at her feet. The Caddy's tires squealed as he turned the corner. Mercy was right behind him.

But the Caddy was faster than her eight-year-old pickup. He turned the next corner, and then zipped around the corner after that. She couldn't keep up. And she was afraid she might throw up—not to mention hit someone. It just was too dangerous to drive so fast in a residential neighborhood.

Praying that wherever he was going, he would get there safely, she slowed. She pulled to the curb, rested her forehead on the steering wheel and breathed slowly through her nose until her stomach settled down.

Then she headed home.

Elena was still there, waiting, looking so forlorn, on the front porch. Mercy pulled into the driveway and ran for the steps. Her sister held her arms out.

Mercy went into them. They held each other so tight. They were both crying.

After a while, they went inside. Mercy told her sister what she'd learned that night from Aleta Bravo.

Elena didn't have much to add. She said their father had told her he was sorry for everything. That he'd been staying right there in San Antonio, but now thought it was better if he went away.

"He was a little drunk, I think, and talking crazy about trying to kill Davis Bravo and ending up shooting Davis's wife. He said he would turn himself in, and then he said he was going to head for the border. None of it made much sense, until now, with what you've told me…"

"Aleta swore she wouldn't press charges," Mercy said. "I believed her. She was honestly sympathetic to what *Papi's* been going through. And she's left her husband. She said he's told one too many lies."

"It's all so damn sad." Elena's shoulders slumped. And then she straightened. "You should call dad, leave a message on his cell, tell him that Aleta Bravo really is okay, that she isn't blaming him or pressing charges."

So Mercy got out her phone and called her father. The call went straight to voice mail, as always lately. Mercy left the message that Aleta was well and had promised not to press charges.

And then, since she had no idea when she might see him again, she added, "I wish you could have waited until I got here, Dad. Because, well, I have something to tell you. Something important. I'm getting married in twelve days, a week from next Saturday. To Luke Bravo. Please don't be angry, Dad. Don't consider it a betrayal of our family. Because it's not. It's…it's love, *Papi.* Real, true love. I wish I could tell you how much I love him. What a good man he is. I wish I could make you believe that everything will be all right if you'll only come home. *Papi,* I know that it's too much to ask, but I'm asking it anyway. Come to Bravo Ridge. At three in the afternoon a week from next Saturday. That's when I'll be married, Dad. It would mean so much if you could be there…"

Was there any more to say? Oh, yes. A thousand things. But she had no idea if he'd even get the message. She hung up.

After that, for a while, she and Elena sat together on the sofa, with Orlando between them. They didn't say much. But then, she and her sister had never needed a lot of words.

Finally, Elena said, "You should go back to Luke."

"Will you be—?"

"Mercy. I'll be fine. Now, go."

He was waiting for her on the veranda, sitting on the top step with Lollie stretched out beside him. He rose when she drove up.

She stopped the pickup and got out and ran up the steps to him. He caught her fast in his strong arms.

"Your father…?"

"He was leaving when I got there, in his car, driving away. I didn't even get to talk to him."

"I'm so sorry, Mercy."

"Your mom?"

"She went up to her rooms. She said what she needed was a stiff drink and a good night's sleep. She can be real practical, my mother."

"But I…I don't understand why she left your father. I mean, I'm no fan of your dad. But at least he told her the truth all those years ago. He admitted he'd had an affair. And he honestly didn't know about Elena."

"I don't think my mom believes that."

"That he didn't know? But *my* mother says—"

"Mercy."

"What?"

"I just don't think she believes him. It's something they're going to have to work out, between the two of them."

"Yeah. All right. I guess so."

"Hungry? You never did get to eat your dinner."

"Yeah. I could definitely eat."

So they went inside. In the kitchen, Luke heated up another plate of food and sat across from her as she ate. Once she was finished, they climbed the stairs together, their arms around each other, Lollie taking up the rear.

In his bedroom, they undressed and got into bed.

He pulled her close against him, spoon-fashion, smoothing her hair back from her cheek and kissing her ear. "We could put off the wedding, if you—"

"No way. We're getting married a week from Saturday, as planned." She wiggled around so she could see his eyes. "Unless you've changed your mind…"

"Are you crazy? Never."

"All right, then. We're getting married. Here at the ranch that your grandfather won from my grandfather."

"Yes, ma'am."

"I love you, Luke."

"And I love you."

"So much."

"More than anything. I want to spend my life with you, Mercy."

"We'll be together, in spite of everything."

He smiled. Even through the shadows of the night she could see the fine curve of his mouth, the flash of his white teeth. "Like Romeo and Juliet, only better."

"Stronger," she added.

"And not dead."

She laughed then, and kissed him hard and quick on that beautiful mouth of his. "It's what we agreed at the cabin. A sacred trust, the two of us. To heal all the ugliness between our families. To make the wrongs, right."

"It's a big job."

"It is. And we're the ones to tackle it."

Chapter Sixteen

"You look beautiful." Luz settled the white veil over Mercy's head, adjusting it so it fell smoothly into place.

Mercy's dress was a long column of sleeveless white satin, with a low V-back embroidered with seed pearls. There were pearls in the tiara that held her veil. She loved the dress, which she'd bought at a wedding shop right off the rack. Eventually, when she and Luke married in the church, she planned to wear it again. That would probably be after the baby came, so if she worked at it, she might even have her figure back by then.

"I'm so glad you're here, *Mami*." She touched her mother's soft cheek. It had been quite a task, convincing Luz to attend. She was so certain her presence would only cause bad feelings on a day that was supposed to be full of joy.

But then Elena had gone to talk to her. Mother and

daughter had made peace, of a sort. Elena had somehow made Luz see that the whole point was the uniting of the two warring families. She'd gotten Luz to understand that the first step toward peace was for everyone to show up at important events. Yes, in the beginning it was bound to be difficult. But over time, the tensions would ease. Someday, they might even all begin to see themselves as connected, as family.

That dream was a long way from fulfillment. But they were only going to get there by taking one step at a time.

Thus, Davis Bravo had said he would be there on Mercy's wedding day, too. And Aleta, of course. Luke's parents remained separated. Aleta was living in the suite she and Davis kept, right there at Bravo Ridge. And Davis had the house in Olmos Park.

Twice since the night she left him, he'd appeared at the ranch house, demanding she come home with him. When she flatly refused, he would beg.

Both times, she had sent him away alone.

Still, he was there today, for the wedding. And apparently behaving himself. All the Bravo sons and daughters were there. Ash and Gabe had brought their wives. And there were a few family friends on both sides, including Doc Brewer, who was getting around with a walker after his hip replacement. And Marcella, who continued to run the office at Cabrera Construction.

Javier had left the running of the place in the hands of his second in command, Carlos Vega. So far, apparently, the company was still doing business, even with Javier gone missing. No one had seen him since the night he showed up at Davis and Aleta's packing his little silver gun.

Mercy had claimed one of the spare rooms near the top of the front staircase for her bride's room. With the door open a crack, she could hear the laughter and chatter floating up the stairwell from down in the front sitting room. She knew who had arrived because every ten minutes or so, Elena would pop in with a report.

"I wish you all the happiness your heart can hold," said her mother. "I wish you a lifetime of loving. And babies. Many babies."

Mercy swallowed down the happy tears. It wouldn't do to ruin her makeup before she even made it down the makeshift aisle between the white folding chairs in the sitting room. "Babies, eh?"

"Sí, mija."

She couldn't resist. She hugged her mother and whispered her secret.

Luz's eyes were round as platters. "No."

"Sí."

"¿Cuándo?"

"In May."

Her mother's eyes filled with tears. She dashed them away and hugged Mercy again.

Elena came in. "You two had better not be crying."

"Of course we're not." Luz sniffed.

"They're ready to start." She grabbed Mercy's bouquet of red roses from the stand on the dresser and her own single long-stemmed red rosebud, as well. "Shall I tell them to go for it?"

Mercy smoothed the satin skirt of her gown, adjusted her veil. "How do I look?"

"Beautiful." Her mother and sister breathed the word in unison.

Then Luz said, "I'll go down and tell them. You two should wait at the top of the stairs. And when you hear the wedding march—"

"We're on it," said Elena. "Go."

Luz slipped away.

Elena said drily, "Can you believe it? Even the sperm donor came."

Mercy flipped back her veil, grabbed a tissue and dabbed at her moist eyes in a dresser mirror. "You've got to stop calling him that."

"No. I don't." She spoke proudly. And she *had* been doing her part to unite the warring families. She and Caleb had put their heads together as newfound brother and sister. The two of them had made it their mission to get the other Bravo siblings on board. They'd done a fine job, dragging brothers and sisters out to a series of dinners and the occasional lunch, where they broke the big news that the Bravos had another sister they'd never even known about. "Only *Papi* is missing." Elena grabbed a tissue, too, and dabbed at her own eyes.

"I just pray he's well. And safe." Mercy met her sister's gaze in the mirror.

Elena nodded. "You're right. I know. You're right…"

"Mercedes." It was Zita, poking her head in the halfway-open door to the upstairs hall.

"Hmm?" Mercy turned to her with a smile.

"There's a man at the kitchen door. He says he's your—"

"*Papi!*" Mercy and Elena cried out at the same time. They grabbed each other, laughing—and crying, too. The news was so huge, there was no way to protect their makeup now.

Zita cleared her throat. "He asks that you come and speak with him."

Elena said, "I'll go." She sent Mercy a glance. "I'll walk him around to the front door."

"No." Mercy shook her head. "He might escape." The sisters laughed together again, more than a little hysterically, through their tears. And then they both gathered up their long skirts. "We'll take it from here, Zita. *Gracias.*"

"De nada." Zita looked at them doubtfully. Which wasn't surprising. They were acting pretty crazy, laughing wildly and sobbing shamelessly at the same time.

"Race you to the back stairs," Elena challenged.

They took off. Zita jumped out of their way with a small yelp of surprise. Long skirts hitched high, they ran along the upstairs hall to the alcove that led to the servants' stairs. Mercy was ahead, since she knew the way. She flew down the stairs, Elena close at her heels.

He was there, waiting, looking so handsome and nervous in his best black suit, his hair like the wing of a raven, his eyes full of love. And worry.

At the sight of the two of them, he opened his arms. And they ran to him. He gathered them both in, hugging them so close in his strong arms.

When they finally pulled back to look at him, they let out a pair of happy screams and grabbed him tight again. He said he loved them and that he had missed them. So very much...

The second time they stepped back enough to look in his eyes, he said, "I couldn't stay away, though I think maybe I should have." He touched Mercy's white veil. "It would be too terrible, I think, to have your father arrested at your wedding."

"Nobody's arresting you," Elena declared. "They would have to go through me first. And they all know me well enough by now that they wouldn't even think of trying it."

From the front of the house, they heard the first strains of the wedding march.

Mercy whispered, "It's time…."

The sisters swiped away tears and straightened their dresses. Elena helped Mercy with her veil and smoothed the ribbons on her bouquet of roses.

Elena asked, "Ready?" When Mercy nodded, she said; "I'll start, then." She went ahead of them, through the door to the central hall.

"*Su novio.* He's a good man, you said…." Her father spoke softly.

"Yes, *Papi.* He's a fine man. And I do love him so."

"Even if he is a Bravo?"

She nodded. "It's not his last name that matters, it's who he is." She touched his chest, over his heart. "In here."

Her father's smile was like a benediction. "All right, then. In spite of everything, I still believe it's time to put the old hatreds away. So I give you my blessing, gladly, such as it is."

"Oh, *Papi.* Thank you. Thank you so much. Now, come on. Walk me down the aisle."

He hesitated. "I think it might be wiser if I didn't go out there with you. It's your day, *mija.* You don't need me here, causing trouble, ruining your happiness."

She bit back a fresh flood of tears. "Please, *Papi.* Don't fail me now. Give me your arm. Take me to my love."

"*¿Es tu cierto?*"

"*Sí. Cierto.*"

He offered his arm at last. And she took it. They proceeded out the door and down the hall.

When they arrived at the wide-open double doors to the sitting room, Elena was already halfway down the red-carpeted aisle between the white wooden chairs.

And Luke was there, at the end of the aisle, near the justice of the peace, with Caleb at his side. Mercy focused on him—on her man. Joy filled her heart to overflowing. He arched a brow at the sight of her father. And then he smiled at her. She thought her heart would burst with love.

Yes, there were gasps from the families and friends at the sight of her father beside her. But no one made a move or uttered a word. They all kept their seats and behaved with proper respect.

Her father took her to the end of the aisle where Luke was waiting. The two men—her father and her husband-to-be—shared a long look and a slow, deferential nod.

Then her dad stepped away to stand with Elena.

There was only Luke—his eyes gazing steadily into hers, her hand in his.

She thought how strange life could be: how love, solid and true, could be born from the deepest hatred. How an enemy could become a friend. And more. So much more.

How some families were born. And some were made—out of kindness and patience and generosity of spirit. Out of love.

The justice of the peace intoned, "We are gathered here together to join this man and this woman in the bonds of matrimony…."

Luke squeezed her hand. Mercy gazed into his beloved blue eyes.

The future was theirs now. They would make it a good one, between them. Through happiness and heartache. Through all the days to come.

* * * * *

Watch for Matt Bravo's story,
A BRAVO FAMILY CHRISTMAS,
coming in December 2009, only
from Silhouette Special Edition.

ALEXANDROS KAREDES, SNOW DUSTING the shoulders of his leather jacket and glittering like jewels in his dark hair, stood at the door. Maria felt the blood drain from her head.

"Good evening, Ms. Santos."

His voice was as she remembered it. Deep. Husky. Perfect English, but with the faintest hint of a Greek accent. And cold, as cold as it had been that awful morning she would never forget, when he'd accused her of horrible things, called her terrible names....

"Aren't you going to ask me in?"

She fought for composure. Last time they'd faced each other, they'd been on his turf. Now they were on hers. She was in command here, and that meant everything.

"There's a sign on the door downstairs," she said, her tone every bit as frigid as his. "It says, 'No soliciting or vagrants.'"

His lips drew back in a wolfish grin. "Very amusing."

"What do you want, Prince Alexandros?"

A tight smile eased across his mouth and it killed her that even now, knowing he was a vicious, arrogant man, she couldn't help but notice what a handsome mouth it was. Chiseled. Generous. Beautiful, like the rest of him, which made him living proof that beauty could, indeed, be only skin deep.

"Such formality, Maria. You were hardly so proper the last time we were together."

She knew his choice of words was deliberate. She felt her face heat; she couldn't help that, but she damned well didn't have to let him lure her into a verbal sparring match.

"I'll ask you once more, Your Highness. What do you want?"

"Ask me in and I'll tell you."

"I have no intention of asking you in. Tell me why you're here or don't. It's your choice, just as it will be my choice to shut the door in your face."

He laughed. It infuriated her, but she could hardly blame him. He was tall—six-two, six-three—and though he stood with one shoulder leaning against the door frame, hands tucked casually into the pockets of the jacket, his pose was deceptive. He was strong, with the leanly muscled body of a well-trained athlete.

She remembered his body with painful clarity. The feel of him under her hands. The power of him moving over her. The taste of him on her tongue.

Suddenly, he straightened, his laughter gone. "I have not come this distance to stand in your doorway," he said coldly, "and I am not going to leave until I am ready to do so. I suggest you stand aside and stop behaving like a petulant child."

A petulant child? Was that what he thought? This man who had spent hours making love to her and had then accused her of—of trading her body for profit?

Except it had not been love, it had been sex. And the sooner she got rid of him, the better.

She let go of the doorknob and stepped aside. "You have five minutes."

He strolled past her, bringing cold air and the scent of the night with him. She swung toward him, arms folded. He reached past her, pushed the door closed, then folded his arms, too. She wanted to open the door again, but she'd be damned if she was going to get into a who's-in-charge-here argument with him. She was in charge, and he would surely see a tussle over the ground rules as a sign of weakness.

Instead, she looked past him at the big clock above her worktable.

"Ten seconds gone," she said briskly. "You're wasting time, Your Highness."

"What I have to say will take longer than five minutes."

"Then you'll just have to learn to economize. More than five minutes, I'll call the police."

Instantly, his hand was wrapped around her wrist. He tugged her toward him, his dark-chocolate eyes almost black with anger.

"You do that and I'll tell every tabloid shark I can contact about how Maria Santos tried to buy a five-hundred-thousand-dollar commission by seducing a prince." He smiled thinly. "They'll lap it up."

* * * * *

*What will it take for this billionaire prince to realize
he's falling in love with his mistress…?*
Look for
BILLIONAIRE PRINCE, PREGNANT MISTRESS
by Sandra Marton
Available July 2009 from Harlequin Presents®.

We'll be spotlighting a different series every month throughout 2009 to celebrate our 60th anniversary.

Look for Harlequin® Presents in July!

TWO CROWNS, TWO ISLANDS, ONE LEGACY
A royal family, torn apart by pride and its lust for power, reunited by purity and passion

Step into the world of Karedes beginning this July with

BILLIONAIRE PRINCE, PREGNANT MISTRESS
by
Sandra Marton

Eight volumes to collect and treasure!

From *New York Times*
bestselling authors

CARLA NEGGERS

SUSAN MALLERY
KAREN HARPER

STORIES OF
STRENGTH

They're your neighbors, your aunts, your sisters and your best friends. They're women across North America committed to changing and enriching lives, one good deed at a time. Three of these exceptional women have been selected as recipients of Harlequin's More Than Words award. And three *New York Times* bestselling authors have kindly offered their creativity to write original short stories inspired by these real-life heroines.

Visit **www.HarlequinMoreThanWords.com**
to find out more, or to nominate
a real-life heroine in your life.

**Proceeds from the sale of this book will be
reinvested in Harlequin's charitable initiatives.**

Available in March 2009 wherever books are sold.

INTRODUCING THE FIFTH ANNUAL
MORE THAN WORDS ANTHOLOGY

Five bestselling authors
Five real-life heroines

A little comfort, caring and compassion go a long way toward making the world a better place. Just ask the dedicated women handpicked from countless worthy nominees across North America to become this year's recipients of Harlequin's More Than Words award. To celebrate their accomplishments, five bestselling authors have honored the winners by writing short stories inspired by these real-life heroines.

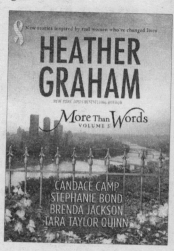

New stories inspired by real women who've changed lives

HEATHER GRAHAM
NEW YORK TIMES BESTSELLING AUTHOR

More Than Words
VOLUME 5

CANDACE CAMP
STEPHANIE BOND
BRENDA JACKSON
TARA TAYLOR QUINN

Visit **www.HarlequinMoreThanWords.com**
to find out more, or to nominate
a real-life heroine in your life.

**Proceeds from the sale of this book will be
reinvested in Harlequin's charitable initiatives.**

Available in April 2009 wherever books are sold.

PHMTW669

THE BELLES OF TEXAS

They're as strong as the state that raised
them. The Belle sisters aren't afraid to go
after what they want, whether it's reclaiming
their ranch or their family.

Linda Warren
CAITLYN'S PRIZE

Thanks to her deceased father's gambling
debts, Caitlyn Belle's beloved High Five Ranch
is in dire straits. Particularly because the
will stipulates that if the ranch doesn't turn
a profit in six months, it must be sold to
Judd Calhoun—the man Caitlyn jilted
fourteen years ago. And Cait knows Judd has
been waiting a long time for his revenge....

*Look for the first book
in The Belles of Texas miniseries,
on sale in July wherever books are sold.*

REQUEST YOUR FREE BOOKS!

2 FREE NOVELS PLUS 2 FREE GIFTS!

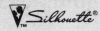

SPECIAL EDITION®

Life, Love and Family!

YES! Please send me 2 FREE Silhouette Special Edition® novels and my 2 FREE gifts (gifts are worth about $10). After receiving them, if I don't wish to receive any more books, I can return the shipping statement marked "cancel." If I don't cancel, I will receive 6 brand-new novels every month and be billed just $4.24 per book in the U.S. or $4.99 per book in Canada. That's a savings of at least 15% off the cover price! It's quite a bargain! Shipping and handling is just 50¢ per book.* I understand that accepting the 2 free books and gifts places me under no obligation to buy anything. I can always return a shipment and cancel at any time. Even if I never buy another book from Silhouette, the two free books and gifts are mine to keep forever.

235 SDN EYN4 335 SDN EYPG

Name _____ (PLEASE PRINT) _____

Address _____ Apt. # _____

City _____ State/Prov. _____ Zip/Postal Code _____

Signature (if under 18, a parent or guardian must sign)

Mail to the **Silhouette Reader Service**:
IN U.S.A.: P.O. Box 1867, Buffalo, NY 14240-1867
IN CANADA: P.O. Box 609, Fort Erie, Ontario L2A 5X3

Not valid to current subscribers of Silhouette Special Edition books.

Want to try two free books from another line?
Call 1-800-873-8635 or visit www.morefreebooks.com.

* Terms and prices subject to change without notice. Prices do not include applicable taxes. Sales tax applicable in N.Y. Canadian residents will be charged applicable provincial taxes and GST. Offer not valid in Quebec. This offer is limited to one order per household. All orders subject to approval. Credit or debit balances in a customer's account(s) may be offset by any other outstanding balance owed by or to the customer. Please allow 4 to 6 weeks for delivery. Offer available while quantities last.

Your Privacy: Silhouette is committed to protecting your privacy. Our Privacy Policy is available online at www.eHarlequin.com or upon request from the Reader Service. From time to time we make our lists of customers available to reputable third parties who may have a product or service of interest to you. If you would prefer we not share your name and address, please check here. ☐

Stay up-to-date on all your romance reading news!

The Inside Romance newsletter is a **FREE** quarterly newsletter highlighting our upcoming series releases and promotions!

Go to
eHarlequin.com/InsideRomance
or e-mail us at
InsideRomance@Harlequin.com
to sign up to receive
your **FREE** newsletter today!

COMING NEXT MONTH

Available June 30, 2009

SSECNMBPA0609